# LEX

## CORA ROSE

# CREDITS

Editor: Angela O'Connell

Cover photography by Michelle Lancaster @lanefotograf

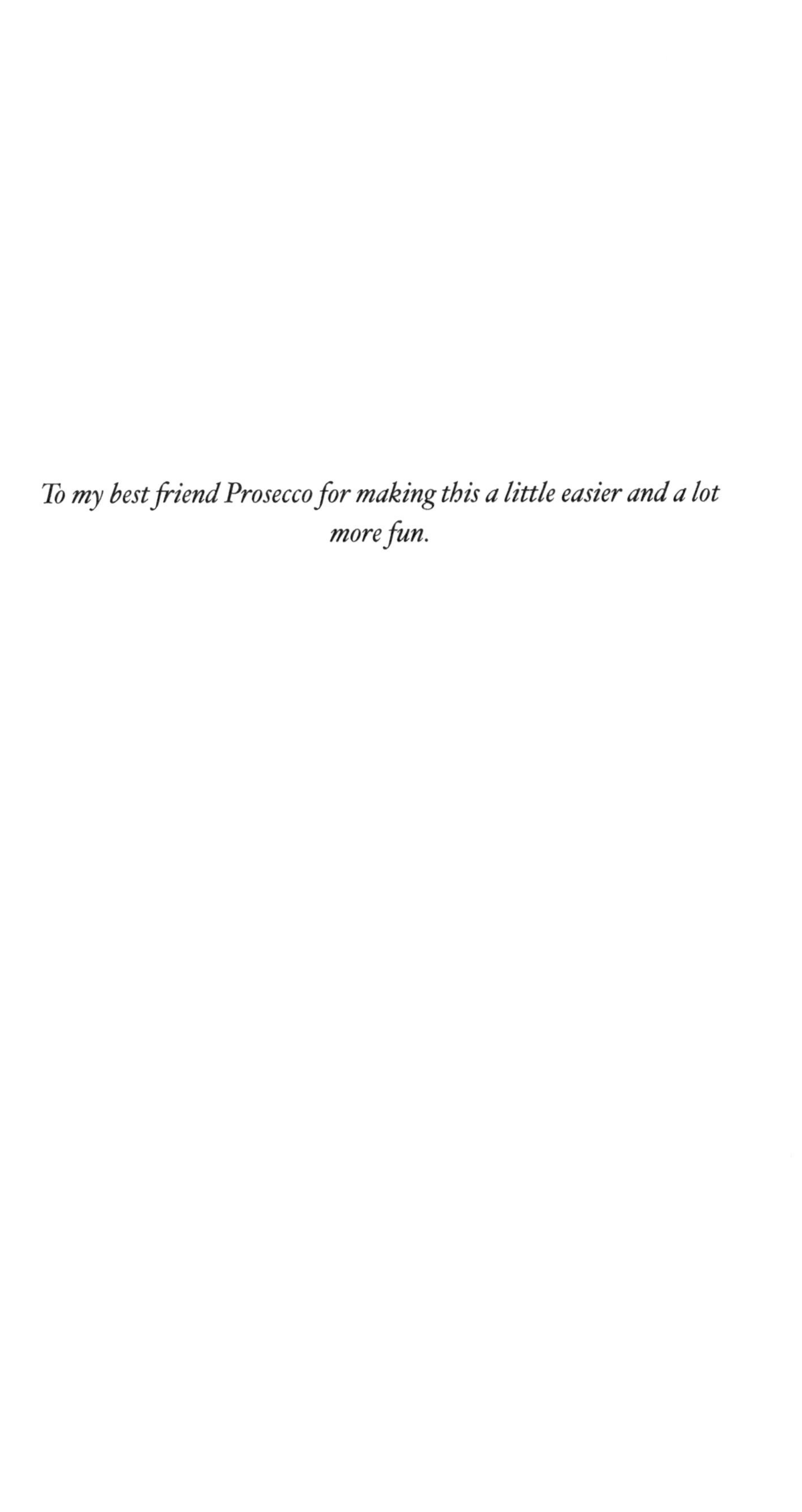

*To my best friend Prosecco for making this a little easier and a lot more fun.*

# INTRODUCTION

The individual characters depicted in this book are fictional and are not meant to represent any particular group, identity, or sexuality. After all, everyone experiences love and attraction differently. This is Lex and William's story. Enjoy!

# PREFACE

Lex, you snarky bitch. I drank copious amounts of wine to write this. You didn't let your story unfold easily.

But I gave you a happy ending anyway, asshole. You deserve it.

So you're welcome.

You can thank me later.

# CHAPTER ONE

## LEX

"Brenda, why are you so wiggly?" I sigh loudly, my gloved hands trying to hold her head still. "You're ninety years old. You should not be moving this much. You're going to break a hip or something."

She wiggles some more, and I purse my lips, trying to apply the last of the hair dye to her bobbing head.

Brenda chuckles a little, her mouth quirking into a sassy smile. "Ninety's not *that* old. Plus, I'll be sitting still when I'm dead. Got to move while I still can."

"Do not talk about dying," I mutter as I squeeze the last of the red dye onto her white hair. "You're going to live another thirty years. I looked it up. It's possible."

She smiles up at me and I blink down at her. I'm not fucking joking. Brenda will live forever if I have anything to do with it. I'm going to go all mad scientist on this shit. I have the goggles and everything. I could probably even manage the wacky hair too if I put some effort into it.

Brenda chuffs a laugh. "You're a hoot, Lex."

I sniff. "Yes, I know I am. I happen to know this about myself. I crack myself up all the time."

She resumes wiggling and I just sigh, letting her. In a way, she reminds me of my best friend, Emery. That guy never sits still. He's a human pogo stick. Maybe that's why I love her so damn much. Is it possible for old ladies to have ADHD? Is that a thing?

"My grandson is so different from you, and yet, you're so alike. I can't wait for you two to meet. You will be electric together," she says after a moment.

Oh, I've heard *all* about her grandson—the elusive asshole who makes no time to visit his grandma. No, that dick just left her here to rot while he travels the United States, living the high life. He's in Florida right now, supposedly doing some accounting work. She has shown me all the pictures he sends. There is no way that man is hunched over a calculator crunching numbers.

Nope, that juicy hunk of man-meat has left his grandma here alone while he fucks his way across the country. I can almost guarantee it because my accountants have *never* looked like *that*.

Listen, here's my issue with this asshole. If I had a family member, anyone like Brenda, I'd never leave them. I would have a hard time even going on vacation. I would probably take them with me...just straight up buy an RV and tote them around.

As it is, I have cameras all over the hallways of this facility, making sure they're all safe. No one is hurting my ladies. If they do, I know of ways to dispose of bodies. With just a press of a button, they'd disappear without a trace, never to be found.

"Well, I don't know if I want to meet him," I reply. But there's no conviction in my voice because the truth is, if Brenda wants us to meet, we'll meet. Like I'd ever say no to her. "Oh, for fuck's sake. Stop scratching your head. Jesus, now look. Your fingers are red. It looks like you've murdered someone."

Her pale blue eyes meet mine and she smiles. "Lex, you're much too bossy. I have seventy years on you. You can't tell me what to do. We've been over this."

"Well, I boss you around anyways, and you always listen to me. Plus, you told me you love me. Too bad, so sad, you're stuck with me. I was love deprived as a child." I gently place a shower cap over the top of her head just as there's a faint knock on the door.

Brenda moves to get up and I hiss at her to sit her ass down. These ladies are all over the place. Goddammit, if one of them falls....

As it is, Brenda's walker sits discarded in the corner. I bought it for her three months ago and she uses it to house her potted plants. I'm a little insulted, to be honest. That thing has fucking all-terrain wheels on it.

I walk the ten feet to the door and wrench it open.

"Vikki, Martha, what a lovely fucking surprise," I say, and Vikki giggles, pulling me into a tight hug.

"How's my boy?" she asks and my heart warms. Yeah, I've never been anyone's boy. My mom was a crack addict who loved getting high more than she loved me, and my dad is in prison for life. I've never met the dude. Honestly, I've felt more parental love in the last six months from these three women than I have in my entire life. So, sue me for sticking around. My therapist says I need to fill that hypothetical affection jar inside of me. And let me tell you, it's pretty fucking full at the moment.

Who would have thought that installing the security cameras and upgrading the Wi-Fi at a senior living facility would lead me down this path to finally finding a family?

Not me, that's who.

"Martha, love the hair," I say, admiring the bright silver locks I'd dyed two days ago. We match now. "I'm dying Brenda's right now. It's blood red."

"How creepy. Can't wait to see it," Martha says and pulls me in for a long hug. When we pull apart, I show them inside, holding onto Martha since she seems a little wobblier these days.

Goddammit, why couldn't I have met them ten years ago? Even a year ago would have been better than this. Why does it feel like each day they grow older and older? What the fuck am I going to do if one of them ever...? I shove the thought away.

Not happening. Thirty more years for each. I decree it.

I make them each a cup of green tea as they settle into their seats, chitchatting about whatever the fuck is going on around here. I've researched this shit and it's the healthiest. I'm trying to get them to commit to being a vegetarian like me, but Martha holds onto meat like a caveman and Vikki gives two fucks about her health.

Brenda is the last holdout. I'm *this* close to bringing her over to the dark side.

Although the other day I heard her whisper filthy things to a piece of steak before she bit into it, so perhaps I'm not as close as I think I am.

"Have you heard about George and Nalda?" Vikki asks,

and I crane my neck to hear from my spot in the small kitchen. Yeah, I'm a nosy bitch. The drama in this place can be fucking nuts. Who knew old people acted like crazed teenagers? "The two of them are finally together now."

"No shit," I mutter to myself, grabbing the cups and bringing them over to the small living area. Each apartment is tiny enough that these folks can move about with minimal effort and with my long legs, I can usually move from the kitchen to the bedroom in less than six strides. The furniture is sparse too. There's just enough to keep them happy but not too much that it becomes a tripping hazard.

As I pass the mugs out, I warn, "Don't burn your tongues, okay? I didn't make it that hot, but...dammit, Brenda, why are you gulping it like that? What did I just say?"

She smiles at me saucily. That little minx, always causing trouble, giving me heart attacks and shit. When you're that old, you don't heal as well. For fuck's sake, yesterday, she told me she wanted a tattoo. I'd about keeled over from the shock of it. I'd told her absolutely not, there's a high risk of infection.

She'd just rolled her eyes. She doesn't take me seriously at all. If she sneaks out and does something wild like that, I may have to resort to extreme measures. I don't know what that would look like yet, but I *will* figure it out. It will have to be enough to deter her, but not actually hurt her. She's getting a tattoo over my dead body.

"Well, good for those two. You're never too old for love," Martha says, ignoring my little rant about safety risks.

"Or to get it on," Vikki adds, blowing into her mug and then sipping at it.

I shudder a little imagining two old wrinkly people fucking as I kick my feet up and eye my phone. I gotta make sure to rinse Brenda's hair in a few. It will take her a hot minute to hobble over to the bathroom too. She moves slower than molasses.

Three months ago, I caved and bought a portable salon chair to use in their bathrooms so they don't hurt their backs when I rinse the dye out. Yeah, yeah, there's a salon in this place, but I do it better, and I give them the wild colors they've all been fawning over.

Tattoos are a no-go, but I'll keep making their hair bright and colorful if they want.

"And did you hear about how Fred tried to hide that prostitute under his bed last week? They're talking about kicking him out now," Martha says.

"Serves him right," Vikki replies. "He should have never shoved that poor lady under there. Treat her with a little respect. At least offer her the closet or the pantry."

I eye the two of them and Martha pats me on the knee. "Enough about them. What have you been up to today, love?"

"Just total world domination," I snark and then nudge Brenda a little. "I hung out with this lady here for a bit. Took her to breakfast. I tried texting you two, but neither of you answered your phones and you didn't answer your doors either."

"We were busy," Martha says, and I raise an eyebrow at them.

"Doing what?"

"I was sewing those pajamas for you and Vikki was listening to that audiobook you gave her."

I swell with happiness that Vikki is actually using the subscription I got her. She was an avid reader up until recently when her eyesight started to go. And of course, as soon as I'd heard, I came to the rescue. I talked with her daughter and got her a simple cell phone with one app on it.

It took her a while to get the hang of it, but now she has her headphones in most days, listening to the books I've downloaded for her. And let me tell you, they are naughty books. I wholeheartedly approve.

I glance down at my phone. "Alright, Brenda, it's time to rinse."

I stand and help Brenda up from the couch, guiding her to the bathroom and into the salon chair.

"You're going to love this," I say as I gently lean her back and rinse the color from her hair.

As I'm watching the water turn from clear to red, Brenda's eyes close and she falls asleep for a bit. She's been falling asleep more often, recently. I don't know what that means, but it makes me fucking nervous. I did all the Googling on it and it seems like it's normal, but I'm not taking any chances. I'm going to get her in to see a doctor soon.

I condition her hair, then rinse it once more, and as I'm massaging the towel over her head, I say, "Alright, lady. Time to wakey, wakey."

She snorts awake with a jolt and blinks up at me.

"You woke me from a *great* dream."

"Do not tell me this dream, Bren. My brain can't handle it."

She grins at me, and I roll my eyes. Let me tell you, I don't embarrass easily, but shit, the things Brenda spewed last week after she'd woken from a nap. I admit I was slightly disgusted, but also intrigued. I do not know the shenanigans Brenda got up to in her past life, but fuck, she seems like she was a force to be reckoned with.

"Let me blow dry you and then we can make you look like the fucking supermodel you are."

It's her turn to roll her eyes to the ceiling, but still, she lets me fuss around with her hair until it's styled just the way she likes.

When we move back into the other room, Vikki is fiddling with the TV remote and Martha is staring at her phone, frowning at the screen.

I help Brenda sit down and then lower myself next to Martha.

"What did you do?" I ask because with these ladies it's always something.

She sighs heavily, the weight of the world on her shoulders. "I swiped on this message from Hannah, and it disappeared. I can't fucking find it."

I pry the phone from her fingers. "Let me show you where it went," I say, pushing a few buttons and then explaining how to retrieve it. She's listening intently, but she won't remember how to do this. This isn't the first time I've explained it. It's why most of my messages sit unread until I arrive at their places, open up the app, and read them out loud.

I don't know why I even bother texting.

Calling is never a sure thing either. Most of the time they don't remember to actually have their phones on them. Or even *on*.

"You're a godsend," she cries, snatching her phone back and staring at the message on the screen.

"Your son got you a phone that is too hard for you to use."

"I know. This is space-age stuff, Lex. *Star Trek* has nothing on this."

I snort a laugh. "It is. I'll research and find something better and easier for you to use."

"Good," she says, turning the phone off and stuffing it in her bra. "Vikki, find us something fun to watch before I die of boredom."

These ladies better stop talking about dying. I can't fucking stand it...makes me anxious.

Vikki eyes me and winks, reading my mind. "We have years, Lexy. Years."

And god, I fucking hope so. I don't want to have finally found my people, only for them to be ripped from this earth. My heart couldn't handle it. My mom died three years ago, and I could give two shits. She was an awful mom and a terrible person. But the thought of Brenda, Martha, or Vikki not waking up one day makes my stomach churn.

Or hell, slowly getting dementia and forgetting all about me.

I've had nightmares about that.

"How about this one?" Vikki asks, pointing to the TV. "Looks raunchy."

I'll watch anything right now. I need to stop thinking about this depressing shit.

Two hours later, I kick my feet off the coffee table and stand up.

"Alright, guys. I've got stuff to do, so I have to get going. Plus, you all need your naps. See you tomorrow?"

"See you tomorrow," they chime, and I bend over hugging each of them before pressing a kiss to Brenda's cheek. I adore them all, but fuck, Brenda is something special. There is just something about her that calls to me on a deeper level.

She and I are soulmates of sorts. If I ever had a mother, a real mother who cared for me the way she should have, she'd have been just like Brenda. She's everything I'd want in a parent—kind, loving, accepting, and just an overall wonderful person.

How she managed to have a grandson like she does, I'll never know.

"Bye," I say.

"I love you," she says softly, and I blink furiously, my eyes stinging.

She told me that two months ago and continues to tell me every time I see her, and I still can't get used to it. It makes my heart palpitate every damn time.

I don't think anyone in my life has said it to me. *Ever.* Until her.

I still don't understand how someone can give that out so freely. It's sacred. But she did. She gave it to me.

"Love you too," I reply, the words always coming out choked.

Well, fuck me. I can never quite get them out without my voice wobbling. For some reason, it just makes me want to sob like a baby.

The truth is, I did sob the first time she said it to me. I made it to my car, grabbed onto the steering wheel, and wept.

But I can't do that every time she says it; I need to keep it together. Lexington Cavanaugh only cries when absolutely necessary. I have Teflon skin. I am a motherfucking lizard person.

"Text me if you need me," I say, and then realize none of them actually will. I don't know why I even bother saying anything. I'll check on them when I get home.

Like I said—video cameras everywhere. Well, except for in their apartments. I draw the line there. I don't want to be a total creeper and I know that Martha walks around without her bra on. She told me so.

My eyes do not need to see that.

As I'm making my way out the door, I nearly stumble into a man hovering in the hallway. He startles a little when I nearly plow into him, and then offers me a soft smile.

"Hi there," he says, his voice rich and smooth. "Um, do you happen to know if Beth is here, or what room she's in? She gave me the wrong room number and isn't answering her phone."

"And you are?" I ask, skeptical of this guy. He's too fucking charming. Never trust a man who smiles this easily or has a voice this sexy. This kind of man robs people blind.

"Oh, I'm her grandson, and this is my son, Daniel."

I glance down at the little brown-haired kid blinking up at me, then I open the door a little and shout, "Brenda, Vikki, where's the new lady at?"

"What did he say? My hearing aid isn't working," Brenda squawks.

"Damn things," Vikki exclaims. "Should just flush them, like cocaine."

I hold up my finger at the man and the boy and then stride over to them, leaning down and saying loudly, "New lady, where she at?"

"Oh, room 133."

"You hear that?" I ask as I make my way back to the door and lean against the frame.

The man nods and extends his hand out toward me. "Thank you. I'm Colin by the way."

I stare at his hand and then slide mine into his. "Lex. So very nice to meet you."

I could fuck this guy. Or he could fuck me. I could go either way, really. I don't discriminate. Although, he seems a little too nice. I usually don't like that in the bedroom. I'd rather people not be so polite while we're getting down to business. He looks like the type to thank someone after sex. I shudder at the thought.

No, I want it dirty and rude.

"Why is your hair that color?" the little boy at his side blurts, and I squat down, so we're at eye level.

"I dye it this color."

"Why?"

"Because I like it. What color should I dye it next?"

He looks up at his dad as if asking for permission and then says, "Blue. It's my favorite color."

"Done," I say, and then hold up my hand for a high-five.

The little fucker slaps my hand kind of hard and I shake it out with a whistle. "Good one, kid."

When I stand back up, Colin is smiling softly at me and... oh, no. *Nope.* Not going there with this guy. This guy wants someone to raise his kid and be a daddy.

I never had a dad, and I definitely don't know how to be one. I will *never* be one.

"You should probably be on your way," I say, nodding toward the exit. "And I have an appointment I can't miss."

Colin agrees, grabbing onto the boy's hand.

"Thanks again and maybe we'll run into each other sometime, Lex."

"Sounds like a plan."

I'm walking away when Colin stops me. "Hey, actually, would you like to exchange numbers? You know, just in case something happens with your grandma or mine."

I let my eyes run over him. "Oh, you're a sly fox, Colin."

He smiles at me, looking much too innocent, and I roll my eyes. "Fine."

I don't correct him that Brenda, Martha, and Vikki aren't

technically my grandmas. For all intents and purposes, they are. They're mine.

I pull out my phone and when we're done swapping numbers, I stroll outside, waving goodbye to Ben who sits behind the check-in counter. His face flushes red when our eyes meet.

I think he has an itty-bitty crush on me. I probably flirted a little too hard with that one when I first showed up six months ago. And, you know, every day since. I can't help it. I'm just a flirtatious guy. The problem is, Ben does nothing for me.

Not that it would stop me. I'd still fuck him. I think he'd let me, too. He's probably a nice, obedient bottom. But I meant it when I said I wanted rude. I want angst. I want long-ing. I want an up-against-the-wall, clothes still on because I'm that desperate for it kind of fuck.

God, it's been a while since sex has made me pant and whine. I want to feel like an animal begging for it. Feral and raw.

Is that too much to ask?

I step out of the facility and the summer heat is almost unbearable as I jog to my car. My pale skin can't handle the rays. I turn as pink as cotton candy if I stand outside too long. Not that there's anything wrong with cotton candy.

I love that shit. Love how it just disappears as soon as it hits my tongue. It's magic.

I pull out my phone and glance at it.

"Fuck," I mutter. I'm going to be late for this job. I'm heading to an office to do some very basic IT stuff that I get paid a shit-ton for.

A wave of panic crashes through me and I start to sweat. But then I gain control, tamp it down, and slow my stride.

They can wait. The man who had called it in was an ass on the phone anyways, demanding this and that. It was a last-minute urgent call that I'd only taken because I'm a nice person.

I'm only rude when it's warranted.

Which happens to be quite often. People are quite awful, really. I learned that lesson early on.

So, yeah, Mr. Walker can wait while I drive my ass across town. Maybe I'll even stop and grab a few snacks. And by a few, I mean I want a fucking mini-mart in my car. I want all the sugary goodness I can buy.

And he'll wait.

Because I'm the best at what I do and he knows it.

# CHAPTER TWO

**LEX**

"You're late," a short, stout man reprimands, a frown on his face. He has sweat beading up on that bald little, round head of his. I have this irrational urge to pluck it right off his shoulders and send it shooting down a bowling lane.

I'm not that late. Only an hour. I spent a lot of time perusing the snack aisle at the gas station. I have a bag full of treats to consume later, and after meeting this fella, I'm glad I didn't rush.

"Why hello to you too," I say with a wide, intense smile. I give a short, mocking bow. "Lex, at your service."

The man grimaces and then turns on his heels and moves toward the elevator. I heft my bag over my shoulder as I follow him.

"I'm Jason, Mr. Walker's assistant. He's unhappy things have been delayed."

"Oh dear, whatever will I do with myself? How will I make it through the rest of my day?" I reply in an exaggerated tone. Mr. Walker, the entitled prick, can suck a fat dick. Not mine, of course, but definitely a big one, and I hope he chokes on it.

Jason steps into the elevator and punches the third-floor button.

I lean against the elevator wall and take him in. Let me tell you, it's not a pretty sight. His shirt is a little too snug on his body, stretching the buttons to near capacity, and there are distinct wet marks under his armpits. He's panting slightly, even though we only walked about twelve strides to the elevator. His little fingers are fidgety, like squirmy centipedes. Sneaky, poisonous fuckers with all those wiggly little legs. I shudder.

"Are you going to die?" I ask. "Because you don't look well, Jason."

"I'm fine," he bites out.

"You don't look fine. You look like you're about one hectic Monday away from flatlining."

The elevator dings and the door slides open, interrupting my professional diagnosis. Jason appears unconcerned about his imminent death, and just turns and walks swiftly down the long hallway. But he should be concerned. He looks very, very stressed and unhealthy.

When we arrive in front of suite 324, Jason opens the door. It leads into a small, empty waiting room, and I continue to follow him through another door that opens to a short hallway of offices.

"A bit eerie back here, huh? Where are all the people?" I ask, noting the absence of life. "Are you running a morgue? Do you embalm dead people in your spare time, Jason?"

"Of course not. This is an accounting firm. We are still getting set up, which is why you being on time was of the utmost importance."

I stop walking and stare at Jason's back. When he realizes I'm not following him anymore, he stumbles a little and makes his way back to me.

"Why did you stop? Come on. We need to move."

He makes it sound like he's running some government agency where lives are on the line. This guy needs a reality check.

I roll my tongue ring across my teeth and fold my arms across my chest. "Jason, I am an hour late to an appointment I squeezed into my tight schedule because I am a saint. Do not berate me like this or I'll leave. And trust me, you don't want me to leave."

He nods curtly, swiping at his forehead with a handkerchief before jamming it back into his pocket. "I apologize."

Now, that's better. I'm no doormat. I start moving again and Jason looks relieved that he doesn't have to fight me on this. His heart probably can't handle it anyway.

"Here is Mr. Walker's office. If you could start in here, that would be great."

I offer a fake smile. I'll start wherever the fuck I want, but I don't say that. I find it's best to not argue with people like him. I don't have the time or the mental capacity to deal with idiots.

"Righto," I say and Jason lingers in the doorway before nodding and disappearing entirely.

Good riddance, sweaty man.

I set my bag down and take a look around, noticing the new carpet and ornate mahogany desk sitting near a large window. A large fake plant rests against a wall with an abstract painting hanging above it. It's fancy but I'm not impressed. I don't trust a person who can't handle the responsibility of watering a real plant once a week.

I squat down and begin pulling out what I need to get the job done when I hear the door open behind me. I just ignore it. If it's Jason hurrying me along already, I will probably reach out, grab onto his ankle, and tug. Watch him fall over like a tiny tree.

Timber, motherfucker.

"Who are you?" a deep voice says above me, and I freeze as a pair of nicely polished black dress shoes move into my vision.

I let my eyes slide up the fine specimen standing beside me. Dark grey pressed pants—a little tight in the crotch, showing me the slight outline of an impressive dick, a white button-up shirt pulled snug over a trim waist and broad chest, a blue tie, and a fitted suit jacket over strong shoulders.

Yes, very nice indeed.

When I get to his face, though, all my hopes of bending him over that fancy desk and railing into him vanish.

Fuck, I would have snacked on him for hours if he wasn't wholly and entirely inedible.

Nope, I can't eat him because the delectable strawberry shortcake standing before me is Brenda's motherfucking grandson.

He's the asshole who cast her away and only texts when it's convenient for him.

Still, she shows him off devotedly and speaks so highly of him. Not that he deserves it.

Our eyes meet and I sigh.

"Shame," I mutter, pushing to a stand. He's about the

same height as me, just over six feet, and I can look directly into his eyes.

Well fuck, he's even better-looking in person. He looks a little older than me and his hair is a gorgeous auburn that literally shines in the light. His jaw is strong and cleanly shaven, and his nose isn't even bent, but there are freckles there. Gah, those innocent freckles and big blue eyes. He's perfect. Like a pretty painting.

"You must be Mr. Walker."

He gives me a clipped nod and hell, he doesn't recognize me, even though I'm sure Brenda has mentioned me. I mean, I know she has, I've overheard the conversations. But Brenda doesn't know how to send pictures on her phone, so the few selfies I have with her are just sitting there.

William Walker has no idea who I am.

But I sure as fuck know who he is, and that is the reason I refuse to shake his hand. Not that he's offering. His cheeks are flushed slightly as he moves around to his wide, overly ornate desk and sits down in his leather chair. Then he folds his hands over his torso and meets my gaze.

"You must be the man we hired to set up the computers."

"I am."

"I'm on a deadline."

"Oh, you don't say?" I drawl with a roll of my eyes. "Well, same, Mr. Walker. But know this, I usually book over a month out. So, thank your lucky stars I squeezed you in."

His eyes flick down my body and then settle squarely on my eyes once more.

"What do you need from me?" he asks, and I pull my lip ring into my mouth, pondering that. Oh, let me see. I'd like very much for you to leave. Not the room but the state. To just disappear into thin air. I don't like competition and I don't want Brenda splitting her time between us. I am very territorial.

I did not just find my person to have her ripped away.

I flick my tongue out and play with the barbell between my lips.

His blue eyes track the movement, and I notice his hands clasp tighter, his knuckles whitening.

Oh, he's a hard one to figure out. Like a puzzle.

Well, let me tell you, I hate puzzles. All those tiny pieces trying to be stuffed into places they don't belong. The worst part is, I always find myself spending hours on them despite how much I hate them. It's a bit of an unhealthy obsession. I can't walk away until the damn thing is all put together.

Do not even get me started on missing pieces. They make me want to overturn tables and burn down buildings.

Fuckers.

"I just need you to stay out of my way," I say, wanting him to go back to fucking Florida and leave Brenda alone.

He eyes me for a long moment and then gives me another clipped nod.

He turns his gaze toward his computer, not realizing that nothing is connected yet and he can't even turn it on. This man is technologically inept. Maybe that's where Brenda gets it from. I wonder if this guy uses his iPad as a drink coaster like she does.

"If you would be so kind as to give me some space, I can work a lot faster. That way you can meet your hypothetical important deadlines your assistant hinted at."

My snark isn't lost on him, and he clears his throat. "I apologize if Jason was rude. We've been...busy."

"Oh, I don't doubt it," I say, turning my back to him and

squatting down, grabbing the equipment I need out of my bag. "Everyone has emergencies, but you have to remember that an emergency on your part does not constitute one on mine."

I look over my shoulder at him, and he nods, unclenching his hands and allowing the blood to flow once more to his fingers. But then it seems to travel up to the tips of his ears because they're suddenly bright red.

He is *not* adorable right now. All this blushing on that pale, freckled skin of his is not endearing.

It's ridiculous and obnoxious.

I force my gaze away before I do something completely in character. Like flirt.

"Now, if you could just shoo, I have work to do."

A fucking poet. That's me.

"I work better without...distractions," I tack on.

He nods and pushes away from the desk, standing abruptly. He towers over me, and my eyes once again travel to his dick. Sorry, not sorry. Those two little orbs have a mind of their own. There is no controlling where they land.

"I should be done in a few hours. Then I'll be out of your hair, and after today, everything will be done remotely on my end."

He nods, eyeing the wall behind me. He wets those pink lips of his and they practically glisten.

"You won't need to come back at all?"

"Nope."

"I see," he replies. "Well, thank you for your time." He moves past me and *my god*, he smells like caramel.

And if you know anything about me, you know I have a slight obsession with anything sweet.

If he was literally anyone else, I'd lick him from dick to

lips right here in his stuffy office. As it is, I'm sweating and trying to keep my tongue from lolling out of my mouth.

But no, I will not do any such thing with this man, especially not with how he treats Brenda.

You mess with her, you mess with me.

Smell as good as you want, William. I will not be licking you.

As soon as the door shuts behind him, I can finally breathe. His scent still lingers, but I push past it. I am not a dog in heat. I can function despite it.

I didn't expect to have such a visceral response to this evil man.

I shove my hand in the pocket of my work bag and pull out my secret weapon. A little camera that most people wouldn't even detect. It rests so innocently in the palm of my hand as my eyes take in the large space.

Where, oh where should I put it?

I snicker to myself.

I'm going to enjoy watching this asshole.

———

A few hours later, my work in William's office is done. It really didn't take me long at all. I made sure all the computers were working and configured correctly. He also wanted video cameras installed in the hallway and sitting room. I don't know why, and I didn't ask because most of my concentration was spent on making sure that the tiny, hidden video camera in his office was working.

He doesn't know I put it there and he'll never find out. I'm just that good.

I lope out of the building with a whistle, feeling pretty damn good about myself.

Yes, I know that hiding a camera in his private space is morally questionable, but what the fuck ever. Let them write "morally questionable" on my tombstone.

I won't deny it. I live in the grey.

I glance down at my phone and pull up the video feed. I immediately see William sitting at his desk holding the card I'd left on his table. He flips it between his long fingers and then runs the back of it across his bottom lip before shoving it into a drawer, almost like it offends him. Wanna bet that's a metaphor? I'm the one he finds offensive. It's probably because of how I look. All my tattoos and piercings make a bold statement and boring people don't like that. They prefer to fade into the dreary wallpaper of their ordinary lives.

I'd wager that William prefers to blend in, just like that fake-ass plant sitting next to him.

I watch as the man who has occupied my thoughts for the last several hours lowers his forehead onto his desk and breathes deeply. Or at least that's what I assume he's doing. I can't quite tell. He could have just dropped dead. But then his head snaps up and he stands abruptly, his chair rolling into the wall.

He strides out of his office with intention.

Hmm, I wonder what he's doing.

I switch to the hallway camera and then the sitting room, watching as he walks through each. Damn, maybe I need to place more cameras around his office so I can see where he's going at *all* times.

I'm a nosy bitch. I don't like not knowing these things.

A moment later, William appears on the sidewalk about twenty feet away from where I sit in my car. He closes his eyes, takes a deep breath, and then adjusts his tie while striding across the street toward a small bakery.

Oh, why, hello there.

Are you a hungry bug? What kind of food do you eat, William? Brains? Small children? Rodents?

I push my way out of my car, shove my phone into the back pocket of my jeans, and jog across the busy street. A car honks at me and I smirk as I waggle my fingers at them.

Thank you so kindly for not killing me on this fine afternoon.

I wrench the bakery door open, and the smell of baked bread and cinnamon invades my senses. Waiting at the back of the line is William, fiddling with his phone.

"Why, hello there. Are you following me?" I say, saddling right up next to him, my breath whispering across the shell of his ear.

I take another long sniff and yep, he smells wonderful. So much so that my mouth begins to salivate.

He flicks his eyes to me and then faces forward. "No."

I run a thumb over my bottom lip and his eyes peek over at me. I'm not sure if he's intrigued or just socially awkward. Like I said, a puzzle.

He's one I'm going to solve. There better not be any goddamn missing pieces. I'll set myself on fire if there are.

"I thought you had a deadline, and yet here you are," I say. He moves forward in line, and I just hover, inhaling him, and generally despising the fact that he thinks he has the right to smell this good.

"I was suddenly hungry."

"Ah," I say, leaning into him a little.

"Well, it just so happens that so am I. I saw this little

bakery and thought, mmm, I could go for a snack," I reply, and he fidgets next to me.

Maybe if I lean in more, I can snag his phone without him noticing and steal it away for a bit. I just have to figure out where he's put it—his back pocket, his front, his suit jacket? Right down the front of his pants? I'll need to let my hands wander to find it.

What a chore.

How ever will I manage this?

My mind ponders it for a bit as we move up in line.

"Since we're just standing here, and small talk is done in this type of informal setting...what's your middle name?" I ask, and he side-eyes me.

"Why?"

"I am just so, so very curious. Like a kitty cat." The truth is, I can do a lot with a middle name, like find little secrets people want buried. If he gives me this, he might as well have given me his social security number and address. By the end of this conversation, I'll have the rights to his firstborn.

We step up to the counter side by side. Our shoulders brush and I let my fingers slip behind him, grazing his ass.

It's a nice ass too. Firm and round and bitable.

He jumps slightly but I keep my gaze forward. He probably wonders if I was the one who touched him so inappropriately, but he won't ask. He'll think he just imagined it. Imagine away, William. Let those thoughts soar.

"Middle name, William. I'm so very curious," I say again when he doesn't give me so much as a peep.

"Bernard."

My eyebrows shoot up and I smirk. "Nice."

"It couldn't be helped," he replies.

"What does it mean?" I ask. "Because a middle name like that has to have some kind of purpose."

"I don't know. It just is."

Hmm, well some research will have to be done. So much research. Maybe I'll ask Brenda and see what she can give me.

"Can I help you?" the woman behind the counter asks, interrupting my tangential thoughts.

"I'd like a cinnamon roll and…" William forces his gaze away from me and clears his throat. "Milk."

Ah, so no brains or rotting corpses. Just milk. How fucking innocent. Like a baby. Well, looks can be deceiving. This man is anything but.

"And for you?" she asks.

"Hmm, that custard-filled maple bar, oh and that cheese Danish." I eye the sweets on the rack and add, "And that pecan bun." I glance over at William who looks at me like I'm insane. "Don't judge. I'm a slut for sweets. This is me showing self-restraint."

He holds out his credit card, but I swat his hand away.

"I got it," I say and scan the card on my phone before he can protest. I'm not taking one thing from this guy. I can buy my own damn sweets and his motherfucking milk.

"Thank you."

"My absolute pleasure," I purr and then take the bag the woman is holding out to us.

I move outside and William follows. I still don't have a clue where that phone of his is, and I think the only way I can get to it is to be extra sneaky.

I can set aside any qualms I have about this man. What I am about to do is for the greater good.

"Hold this," I say, handing William the bag full of goodies. He takes it without hesitation and continues to follow me. I spot a small alley two stores down and it's the perfect hiding spot. When we reach it, I grab onto William's tie and drag him into the enclosed space.

"What—?" he asks, but his words are cut off by my lips pressing against his.

"Mmmph," he murmurs as his entire body stiffens and slams into the brick wall behind him.

I probably should have pondered for a moment about consent and whether or not this guy is into men. He could be adamantly against it. But, then again, he isn't immediately pushing me away like I'd expect him to do if he was affronted or grossed out. Which only makes my job of finding his phone easier. He won't notice what my hands are doing.

I move my mouth against his and inhale deeply. He still smells like a donut. I want to slide my tongue into him for a taste. I press my body against his and feel a hard bulge in his nether regions that's definitely *not* his phone. My, William, what a big dick you have.

As I nibble my way across his lips, I realize that he isn't moving. It's like he's frozen solid.

Why the hell is he just standing so awkwardly? I mean, I've kissed some weirdos before, but I've never kissed someone this stiff and unyielding. I might as well be making out with the brick wall behind him.

I wrench my mouth away from his and meet his wide-eyed stare.

"Why are you so bad at this?" I ask.

It really is an anomaly. This man exudes sex, he's clearly hard, and yet, he kisses like a dead fish.

His eyes widen even more, his cheeks flaming. "I've never...I'm..."

"Oh, my *fuck*," I mutter, realization dawning. "Do *not* tell me..." I gasp as he eyes the ground and gnaws at his lip nervously. I use my finger to gently lift his chin and force his gaze to mine. "Was that your first kiss?"

His entire face is crimson now, and my heart gallops in excitement. Oh, this is so surprising and much, much too good not to use. And I will use it. I have no issues doing so. Who said morals were any fun?

"Don't be embarrassed," I whisper, reaching up and straightening his crumpled tie. "I think you could be fabulous at it with a little practice."

He swallows, his Adam's apple bobbing. "I should go. This wasn't...I wasn't...."

I press into his hard body again, my hands smoothing across his chest, and ah, there it is, the phone I should have been searching for all along. I got a tiny bit distracted, but I'm back on track now. I slip it from his coat pocket as I let my lips brush his once more, for good measure.

I mean, this isn't torture. I'm not kidding myself. I'm enjoying this more than I want to.

"Should you really go? Or perhaps, we should practice a bit more?"

He lets out a small huff of air and I swear I hear the slightest whimper.

"Perhaps we should try with some tongue...get a good taste of each other."

Oh yes, my dick likes that suggestion very much. A little hate tongue-fucking. I'd like that with a side serving of cum.

"I can't. I need to go back to work."

"Scared?" I taunt and he swallows.

"Yes."

Oh. Well, that is not what I was expecting. Vulnerability. He wears it so well. It makes him...likable.

Oh dear.

I step back, needing to regain some of my composure before I do something completely out of character. Like try to reassure him.

"Well, I don't feel like being the big bad wolf today, Mr. Walker, so off you go. Maybe I can eat you another day."

He stumbles slightly and then strides past me with my damn food still clutched in his hands.

I will not let a perfectly good pastry go to waste.

"Oh, William," I call, realizing my faux pas of using his first name, not that his brain is functioning properly enough to catch it. Thank god.

He turns to face me, his cheeks still delightfully red.

"I need my motherfucking sweets."

He wets his mouth, and my eyes are drawn to his plump pink lips.

"No, no. Not that," I say, and then point to the bag in his hand. "My food."

He looks down and it takes him a minute to catch onto what I'm saying before he's striding back toward me and thrusting the bag against my chest. It squishes against me, and I groan my disappointment.

There goes my custard donut.

"Here," he says and then ambles away, just his milk clutched in his fingers.

"What a fucking waste," I say, watching his tight ass disappear around the corner.

I stride to my car, peeking inside the bag, and see that yes, my donut is crushed. But of course, I still eat it. I lick it right off the side of the paper bag. No way I'm letting that go to waste. He could have pulverized it in a blender and I'd still suck it up with a straw.

I pull out my phone and pull up the feed from his office, but he's not there. He never went back. So, William lied. Huh. Puzzles and pieces. I hate this shit. It makes me crave answers.

I reach down and let my fingers slide against his phone.

At least I have this.

William Bernard Walker, Lex is coming for you.

# CHAPTER THREE

**LEX**

"Where you off to?" Emery asks me, shifting in his seat and clacking away on my laptop. He's supposed to be working on my business accounting, but I know he's been perusing Instagram and then Reddit for a few hours. It's a good thing I like this asshole. Sometimes I think I could get my shit done in half the time.

In fact, I know I could, but I love him like a brother. So, I just let him take his sweet ass time.

I will keep him around forever and always.

"Hanging with the ladies, per usual," I reply, grabbing my laptop and stuffing it into my satchel.

"Jesus, they take up all your time," my best friend says, pulling a sucker from his pocket and shoving it into his mouth. He sees me eying it and waves me off. "Don't even ask for one. You'll just be disappointed. They're sugar-free."

My eyebrows rise at that. Well, damn. His boyfriend has

managed to do the impossible. He's weening Emery off sugar. He's even more addicted to the stuff than I am.

And I have a very unhealthy obsession.

Hence my dreams about William last night—unwrapping him and eating that thick dick of his. I wonder if there are freckles there too. I'd count them with my tongue.

"I spend all my time with them because you're too busy for me now that you have August," I tell him, wrenching my mind back to reality. I am not going to think about William's dick for another second.

Emery eyes me and smirks. "Yeah, August keeps me busy. So fucking busy."

"I bet he does," I reply with a waggle of my eyebrows as I throw my satchel over my shoulder. "Will you be done by the time I get back?"

"Of course. I took my medication today. I am ultra-focused. Wild stallions couldn't tear my focus away."

He squirms in his seat and then pulls out his phone, playing some game on there.

Oh yes, the amazing ADHD medication he takes. I'm convinced that it works only half the time. If this is him on meds, you don't want to see him without. I guess I should be happy he even made it over here and didn't get side-tracked at the Jamba Juice. That's happened before.

"Whatever works, Eminem. You know, you and August are welcome at my place anytime. You still have a key."

"Yes, well, we would hang out here more often, but you'd just watch us creepily. It makes August nervous. Plus, I don't want you to see his fantastic ass. That's all mine."

"He has nothing to be nervous about. I'm harmless."

Emery points his sucker at me. "You know that's not true."

I hum under my breath. "I'm harmless most of the time," I amend.

There. I can be an adult about this. The truth is, I do miss my best friend. Ever since he moved out, I rarely see him. August consumes all of his time. But I get it, sort of. If I had an August, I'd walk around all day with my dick in his ass. He'd never escape.

"We could hang out tonight if you want," Emery says. "Just text me when you're done with work, and we can meet up."

I eye him and know he's feeling sorry for me.

"No thanks. I have other plans."

I don't have other plans, other than spying on William to see what other little secrets he has. Because let me tell you, that phone of his revealed nothing. I couldn't even hack into it. All the user errors William should have made, he didn't. Plus, he has no social media accounts that I can find and no online presence. It's pretty impressive, actually. I couldn't find anything about William the easy way. So, I'll just have to return his phone and find another way to figure this man out.

I have all sorts of tricks up my sleeve and I'm not giving up yet.

I will find dirt on William and use it to my advantage.

He needs to be taught a lesson on how to treat his precious family members.

I'm petty like that.

"See you later, Eminem," I call over my shoulder, but receive no response because he's hyper-focusing on some shit on his phone—probably naked pictures of August.

I lock the door behind me, jog down to my car, and make my way over to the senior living facility.

"Hi Ben," I say, waggling my fingers at him.

He blushes as I sign in and walk down the hallway to

Brenda's room. I don't stop to flirt though like I normally do. I have plans and I don't want Brenda to think I've stood her up.

I push her door open, and skid to a stop. Because there *he* is, looking fresh and fucking sexy.

What a surprise.

"Well, look who it is," I say dramatically, dropping my satchel near the door and striding through the small room where Brenda sits with her grandson, William.

"Shit," he mutters so softly I almost miss it. But oh, I don't miss it. I hear it clear as day.

I turn to Brenda, "Were you ever going to tell me he was home?"

She just smiles coyly. "I am old and forgetful, Lex."

"Sure, sure. Well, hello there, Mr. Walker. What a *nice* surprise," I declare, beaming at him. His freckled cheeks turn positively cherry red and it's delightful. He's like a jelly donut.

He flexes his hands and glances everywhere but at me. I want to worm my way into that brain of his and take a good look at what he's thinking.

"Lex," Brenda says, grinning. "I'm so glad you're here! This is my grandson, William. William, this is Lex, the one I told you all about."

He looks stunned. "*This* is Lex?"

"Ah, don't be such a spoilsport, William," I say. "You must have heard *all* about me. Or were you not really listening when Brenda called you all those times to tell you about her day?"

He clears his throat and pops his knuckles. I'm not sure if he's just nervous or wants to crack his fist across my cheek. God, he's so full of surprises. I have no idea what he'll do next.

It's intriguing and I hate it.

"Can I speak to you, please?" he says, standing up and gesturing toward the door.

I cock my head and run the tip of my tongue across my upper lip.

"I think that can be arranged," I say, and Brenda looks almost giddy.

Oh, she can zip that right back up. I may have kissed this man, but that is a far cry from a relationship.

I don't do relationships. For obvious reasons. Brenda knows this. We've had long discussions about it. She always pats my knee and tells me *there is someone out there for you, Lex*, and I just bob my head because I don't want to hurt her feelings.

But, no Brenda, there is no one out there for me. That's not a thing that happens in real life. At least not for people like me.

"We'll be back, Bren. Your grandson has something important to say, I'm sure." I follow William out of her room and down the hallway.

When we reach the restroom, William opens the door and gestures for me to enter.

"Oh dear. You've read me all wrong. I'm not in the mood to suck cock at the moment," I say as I step inside, and he shakes his head.

"I'm not...that's not what this is," he says, flustered.

We step inside the bathroom and the door swings shut.

"It's not? Oh, well then Mr. Walker, you have me all confused."

"It's William."

I lean my back against the tile wall and purse my lips in

thought. "Of course it is. I can do all sorts of things with your name. Bill, Billy, Will, Wilhelm."

His cheeks darken once more and it's intoxicating. I could get drunk off of those blushes.

"Stop."

I smirk, taking in his vibrant eyes. They're like a haze rolling in over the ocean—so full of mystery.

"Willy," I can't help but add.

He narrows his gaze slightly. "You can call me William."

"I think Willy is more suitable. It's..." I slide my eyes across his broad chest. "Fitting."

His eyes are mere slits now. "Why are you here with my grandmother?"

"I'm here with *Brenda* because she's my friend. I've spent every day with her for the past six months, which you'd know if you listened to her when she calls. But we all know how very *busy* you were...on the other side of the country."

His jaw grinds, but those blue eyes betray him, because he's sneaking peeks at my mouth.

I don't blame him. It's fabulous. I can do things with my tongue that would make him pass out. What we did in that alley was child's play.

"I was away on business. It couldn't be helped."

"Oh, men like you..." I say, leaning into him, suddenly angry. "You have everything, the *fucking world,* and you squander it."

A knuckle pops again and I dare him with my eyes to punch me. I'd like that very much. He may be bulkier than me, but I can fight dirty. I've had so much practice.

"Lexington," he whispers, and for some reason, my arms break out in goosebumps. How does he know my full name?

And why does that make my dick hard? Bad dick. "I'll call security."

"Oh, please call away. They won't mess with me. Bruce, the big man out there, he and I are friends. Very good friends."

He takes a step closer, so close that I can feel his breath across my mouth and, my god, my entire body thrums with energy. He's like lightning on a summer night—all heat and electricity.

So fucking beautiful, and so very, very dangerous.

"Lexington," he says again softly, his eyes tracing my mouth.

I refuse to look away, despite my entire body nearly trembling.

"I'm not leaving," I mutter and his eyes snap up to mine. "I refuse."

I run a finger up his arm, trying to control this wayward situation. I gently grasp his chin, his breath stilted against my fingertips. "I finally found something I want. And like hell I'll give Brenda up. You don't know the things I've gone through. I don't crumple so easily, William. I rise to the occasion. Don't test me. *You* should leave."

His pupils dilate and fuck, I could lean in and kiss him again. Just bite down on those angry, scowling lips, and make him fucking bleed.

"You're a hard one to read, Willy. Especially because you barely say a word..."

He blinks as if pulled from a trance and wrenches his chin from my hand, taking a step back.

"Are you after her money?"

"Oh Willy-Billy," I taunt. "You know nothing. I don't want her money, nor do I need it."

"Then what do you want?"

Oh, there is a list. Love, friendship, safety, security. But I don't utter any of it. I just stare at him.

"I monitor her accounts."

"Oh dear. I'm *so* afraid."

He shifts on his feet before me, and I roll my eyes. "If I wanted it, I could take it, Willy. None of your password bullshit would help you. But that's not why I'm here. Brenda is important to me, and you will take her away from me over my dead body."

Like hell I'm giving them up. They're mine now.

Come and take them, asshole.

William's countenance darkens slightly and he moves toward me once more. Suddenly his fists are on my shirt, crumpling it in his hands. I'm pressed up against the wall and oh, my dick takes notice. It stands right up at attention.

Hello there, William, all aggressive and murdery—it's so contrary to the innocent milk act from earlier. It sort of makes me want to turn around and bend over for him.

"Kiss me," I whisper because I want to see if he tastes as good as he smells.

He doesn't even hesitate. He crashes his lips into mine and I grab the back of his neck and suck on his plump lower lip.

"Open your fucking mouth," I pant against him, and his lips part slightly.

Such an obedient, angry man.

My tongue darts inside, rubbing against his, and hell, he tastes like black licorice. What would his dick taste like? Probably like a strawberry Pop-Tart.

His grip tightens on my shirt, holding me roughly in place as he breathes into me. He's a terrible kisser but he tastes like a fucking candy store, and it keeps me planted right where I am, devouring his mouth.

I arch my hips against his and he groans lowly. My entire body tingles from the sound and I open my eyes to see his closed tightly, his brow scrunched up in concentration.

This fucker is thinking too hard about this.

I lower my hands, grabbing onto his ass and pressing my thigh against his hard cock again, and his face slackens as he groans louder.

Better, much better. Let go a little, William. Chill the fuck out. This isn't calculus.

I slant my head and deepen the kiss, trying to guide him. The wet sound of our mouths is making me unreasonably horny.

I could go all the way right here, right now. I even have an emergency lube packet in my pocket.

But I don't get to do any such thing because he abruptly pries his mouth away.

"Wa—wait. *Wait*," he says, breathless. His lips are so swollen they almost look bruised, wet and shiny from our saliva.

"I need a break. A break," he says, his words on repeat.

My chest heaves from it all. I was not expecting this when I came in here. Not at all. How very surprising, in such a good way.

"Why?"

He shakes his head swallowing loudly. "I'm...close."

My eyebrows shoot up and then I nod, impressed. Why yes, I am just *that* good.

"You have terrible stamina," I say, pressing a shaking hand against my throat.

"I know. Fuck," he says and then slowly unravels his fingers from my shirt.

"Your kissing still sucks big dick, by the way," I tack on because he looks much too hot, and I need to bring him down a notch or two. For my mental health. I've never been this affected by another man before. I don't know if I love it or hate it.

He blinks rapidly and presses his palm against his crotch. "I just need more practice."

"That can be arranged," I blurt without meaning to, and yet I regret none of it.

It seems I don't hate it all that much. Apparently, I want to keep right at this, despite the fact that he just accused me of possibly stealing from Brenda.

The gall of this obnoxiously sexy man.

William swallows loudly and takes another step back, his hands trembling slightly.

My eyes drag down his chest and land on his straining dick. It presses out from his pants, and from what I can see, it's the perfect size. I could sit on that. No complaints. He'd hit my prostate every time.

"Stop it," he mutters, his cheeks flaming.

"Make me," I reply, and William runs a hand over his face, his breathing still haggard from our make-out session.

"This is getting out of control," he says suddenly. "I just meant to talk to you...not do...*that*."

A laugh escapes me because if he thinks this is out of control, he ain't seen nothing yet.

"Oh, sweet William Bernard, I am going to fucking wreck you if you think this was crazy."

His eyes widen and he clutches onto the door handle, moving to pull it open. I stop him, the words tumbling out of my mouth before I can stop them. "Come to my place tonight and we can practice."

"Practice?" he asks, even though he knows *exactly* what I mean.

"Kissing, fucking, whatever you want. I am an extremely good teacher. Very patient."

He swallows roughly and shakes his head. "You have an ulterior motive."

"Of course I do," I reply. "Don't we all?"

He doesn't trust me, which is fair. I don't trust me most days.

He moves to leave, but I stop him once more, my hand on his firm bicep.

"Before I forget." I reach into my back pocket and hand him his phone.

He swipes it from my grip. "Where did you find this?"

"I didn't find it," I say with a roll of my eyes. "I stole it right before you squished my donut to smithereens."

He blanches. Obviously, he's used to people lying to him. He won't find that with me. I always tell it like it is. No matter how bad it hurts. "Oh, get over it. I couldn't hack into it anyway. You're harder to figure out than I thought, which is...frustrating. And your phone is equally as annoying. Also, who doesn't have social media in this day and age? Are you secretly a vampire who is one million years old and hates the internet? Or perhaps you're in witness protection?"

He clutches his phone so tightly I'm surprised it doesn't crack in his palm.

"Just...stay away from me. And more importantly, stay away from my grandma."

But his eyes flick down to my lips because he just can't

help himself, and I smirk. "Oh, that's not going to happen, William. I'm not going anywhere."

I wrench the door open, step past him, and move into the hallway. "My place, tonight. Bring a change of clothes, just in case you come all over yourself during our session."

"Not happening," he replies.

Oh, he is talking out of his ass right now. He is *so* going to show up at my place tonight, whether he wants to or not.

I reach into my pocket and pull out a pen. Grabbing his hand, I scrawl my name and address onto the inside of his wrist.

"I'm home by nine. Don't be fucking late. You and that mouth of yours need a lot of help."

He stares at my writing across his skin and then meets my stare, but I don't dilly-dally. I just turn on my heel and head back to Brenda's room. Life is short, and I don't need to spend my time here arguing with William—as enticing as that may be.

When I make it back to her room, I see her sitting on the couch, her head leaning back with her eyes closed and mouth open. Always fucking napping. That's not a bad sign, is it?

"Bren," I say and her eyes pop open and a small smile lifts her lips.

"Hi, Lex. You took a while out there. I missed you."

Gah, my heart.

"Yes, well I got a bit sidetracked," I add as I sink down next to her and pull her into a hug.

She holds me tightly for a moment and then lets me go, her hand brushing my cheek. In my peripheral, I see William sinking in the chair opposite us and I can feel those blue eyes on me.

Look all you want, Willy. I'm not fucking leaving.

"Well, you two were sidetracked for *quite a while*," she says, smiling at William who just continues to watch me.

"William was having trouble...processing some things. I had to really spell it out for him...with my mouth."

William is blushing again and Brenda's eyes positively sparkle. There's no pulling wool over her eyes. She's too observant. She knows exactly what happened inside that bathroom. You can read it all over William's face.

"I bet you did." She leans into me. "Told you. Electric."

Well, she's not wrong. William kisses like a sock puppet, but I still got hard as a rock.

"Are Vikki and Martha heading over?" I ask, trying to divert the subject because I refuse to have an erection in front of these ladies. They would never let me live it down. I don't embarrass easily, but I know if that were to happen, I'd just die.

And I'm not fucking dying until I get another piece of William.

I need to see if that was a one-off. That desperation I felt, the way my body vibrated with need. Will that happen every time or was it only in the heat of the moment? An experiment needs to be done immediately.

"Not sure," Brenda says. "Though I would like for them to meet William. He's been gone for so very long."

"Ah, why yes he has been," I mutter, giving William the evil eye. Because as sweet as he tastes, he did leave Brenda here while off doing who knows what. Although I very much doubt he was fucking his way around Florida, not with the way he kisses. He was probably crammed into a small room crunching numbers all day. But still.

He left her.

"Why don't I go get them and we can grab brunch? Mimosas and crepes. Sound good?" I ask.

Brenda glances over at William and my jaw clenches. She doesn't need to look to him for permission. This man is interfering with our well-established dynamic, one that I've come to rely on.

William, all up in my business, is going to ruin things, and it makes me want to ruin him.

"Fine. William can join as well," I grind out because I know she won't leave when he's here. I don't want her to stay inside all day, it's not good for her. These ladies need to get out and move their legs. If they don't, they can get blood clots. I've looked it up. It's a thing.

William folds his hands on his lap, not answering right away. I glower at him until he looks away and nods his agreement.

Good boy, Willy. I didn't want to have to do something drastic. Like call my friend Diablo. He's much scarier than me.

I stand up and clap my hands together. "Right-o, I'll be back with Martha and Vikki and then we'll go."

I stride out of the room and down to Martha and Vikki's rooms, hurrying them along because I don't trust William to not derail my plans in some way.

He's nefarious in his own, quiet way. I can tell.

We make it to the restaurant in one piece—the five of us crowded into my car like clowns at a circus.

I would have preferred if William had driven separately, but Brenda wanted him with us, so who am I to argue? And of course, William has this ridiculous sports car that's so low to the ground Brenda would never be able to get out of it. So I drove because my automobile is sensible. I may even upgrade to a minivan because it will be easier for them to slide in and out of. That's how committed I am to this.

The nerve William has to accuse me of being here for the money, pfft. It's absolutely insulting.

"We'll have five orders of crepes and mimosas all around," I say when the waiter comes to our table to take our order. He eyes me up and down rather obviously, and I think that maybe if it weren't for William watching me, I'd leave him my number on the back of a napkin. Or perhaps meet him in the bathroom for a quick blow job.

But of course, I don't do any of that. I gotta keep my eye on William. He's much too quiet. I don't trust the quiet ones.

"Actually, I'd just like a water and some wheat toast," William interjects, and all eyes swivel to him.

What the fuck? See what I mean? My eyes need to be on him at all times. Because...toast and water?

I mean, I like to manage the ladies' sugar intake but damn, I don't even go that far.

"What the hell are you ordering, Willy? What planet are you from?"

"It *is* odd," Martha interjects loudly. "Who wants that healthy shit when you can have Nutella crepes?"

I flick my hand at Martha as if to say *see* and arch an eyebrow as Vikki tears open a sugar packet and upends it into her mouth.

Motherfuck, I need to monitor her better. She will end up with type 2 diabetes if she keeps that up.

"Live a little, William," Brenda says softly, and I arch my other eyebrow at him. I learned that from my friend Amanda. It's amazing what miracles the eyebrows can work in the art of persuasion.

His cheeks flush slightly, and he gives a clipped nod. "Fine. I'll have the crepes instead."

"Good man," I say, leaning back and grabbing a single-serve cup of vanilla creamer, opening it, and pouring it into my mouth. Because why the fuck not? It's delicious.

William looks horrified. Oh, he has no idea. Vikki makes out with the entire basket of creamers before she leaves, just dumps them right into her purse, and Martha steals a fork each time we come. Brenda pretends to be an angel, but I see her licking her plate sometimes.

I can't wait to see William's expression when he sees her do that.

I toss a creamer at William, and it hits him square on the chest before falling onto his lap.

"Drink up," I smirk.

He sets the miniature cup on the table and Brenda swipes it, her eyes twinkling.

"Grandma, no," William says, but she just ignores him, pouring the contents into her mouth.

That horrified look is back on his face, and I feel incredibly pleased with this turn of events. Suddenly, I am so happy he's here. I like to watch him squirm.

"Don't worry, Willy," I say. "I monitor their intake. We have guidelines they have to follow."

"Damn right we do. And this one is always nagging too," Martha says, upending another sugar packet into her mouth. *"Only five packets, Martha,"* she says in a high-pitched voice that is not at all like my own. "I tried to tell him ten is more reasonable, but he won't fucking budge."

Vikki pockets a spare fork and isn't even sly about it, causing William to gape. When the waiter knowingly replaces the creamer and sugar packets ten minutes later, William almost slides underneath the table.

He is positively mortified, and I delight in it.

"You're despicable," he whispers to me as we leave the restaurant. He has a small bit of Nutella right on the corner of his mouth, so I brush it away with my thumb.

His breath hitches when I lick it clean.

"I am a fan favorite, Willy. You're just a boring piece of ass."

He huffs, his cheeks red, and I lean into him. He smells like vanilla beans.

"Be that as it may, come over tonight for your lesson."

"No. Not happening," he says, his fingers brushing mine. An electric current zings up my arm causing me to shudder.

Hmm, maybe not a one-off then.

Shit.

"Be there, William. Don't make me hunt you down. I will find you. I have my ways."

He clears his throat and I paste a smile on for Brenda who is wobbling toward us. I lengthen my stride and grab onto her.

"You need to hold onto my arm, Bren," I chastise.

"I know, I know, but you were busy." She gestures to William and I roll my eyes, because, yes, I may like kissing him, but we aren't getting married.

I don't do relationships. They're...messy. And they make me all...

Weak. I become weak and I hate it.

"I'm never too busy for you. And how many times have I told you, you need your walker? I even bought you that nice one that works on all surfaces."

"I'm fine," she says, reaching out and placing her hand on William's arm, and my stomach clenches.

Because he is her *actual* grandson. I'm just some kid who wandered into her life six months ago and dyes her hair and sits with her while she watches TV.

Shit.

I am utterly replaceable now that William is back.

"Better hold onto Vikki. She downed that alcohol like a fucking sailor," Martha says, stomping off toward the exit.

I reach back and grab onto Vikki before she tumbles over and breaks a hip, and then lead them out to my car. The entire time I'm dropping them off, I wonder how best to play this.

But I'm really at a loss. I have no idea how to play this particular game.

William is the wild card I never expected.

# CHAPTER FOUR

WILLIAM

I swear to all that is holy, I thought I was asexual. For thirty years I've walked through life not feeling any type of sexual interest in others. Sure, I've found people pleasing to the eye but I've never felt the strong desire to touch them or have them touch me. I was happy with just myself and my hand. Sex seemed sort of like a nonissue and I was perfectly content like that. It was just my form of normal and I'd never really put that much thought into it.

But now I'm thinking about it. In fact, it's all I can think about. The minute Lex strolled into my life, it was like a lightning bolt straight to my dick, like Frankenstein's monster was awoken in my pants.

When I saw his lithe, tight body kneeling on the floor rustling around in his duffle bag, all silver-blond hair and painted black nails...and those piercings, *my god*. Then when he looked up and I saw his face, it was all over for me. My dick perked right up.

It saluted him with the recognition he deserves, and it hasn't really gone down since. I've jacked off more in the past twenty-four hours than I have in my entire adult life.

Maybe I'm not asexual after all? Or maybe I am, but with just one small exception? Maybe I'm in that gray area. I don't know. All I know is that I wasn't interested in being touched, and now, all I can think about is Lex touching me. Lex kissing me. Lex throwing me up against that alley wall and...stealing my goddamn phone.

Fuck, why him? Why does it have to be him? He's so infuriating with his smug attitude and straightforwardness. He has no right to be that hot.

He's fire, and I'm a suicidal moth.

I know he's bad for me, but I can't stay away.

It's why I'm outside his apartment right at this moment, despite all of my better judgment. This man eats sugar packets and drinks mini-creamers before eating a lunch consisting of chocolate and alcohol. It's disgusting and juvenile. What's next, individual jam packets?

And yet here I am, salivating and fantasizing about sticking my tongue in his mouth, again.

My phone rings in my pocket and I pull it out. Grandma's name pops up on the screen and without a second thought, I swipe at it.

"Hey," I say softly.

"Hi, William. It's your grandma," she says, and I bite back a smile because she doesn't seem to get how these smartphones work. She still writes me the occasional text with her name at the bottom of each one.

"I wanted to just call and say goodnight," she says.

I look at Lex's door and move away from it. I can't fucking think when I'm this close to him, even when he's behind a wall.

"Is everything okay?" I ask, concern lining my tone. Lex is right, I've been gone for months, away from her, and I still feel guilty about it. I'd missed out on time with her and I wonder if I did the right thing. There are times I think it may have been a mistake.

"Of course, William, I just wanted to hear your voice before I go to bed."

I sigh and then run a hand through my hair. "How about I stop by tomorrow and we can grab a bite to eat?"

"I'd love that. Now tell me, where are you?" she asks, being her usual nosy self. "Busy night?"

I glance at Lex's door and wince. There is no way I'm telling her where I am. She has been on me about Lex for months. *Lex is so handsome. Lex is so funny. You'll love all of his tattoos.*

Well, she was absolutely correct. I have a bit of an addiction to this man. She must have some magical grandma intuition.

"Nowhere," I lie.

She huffs because she knows. I mean, she didn't raise this shy, quiet kid and not know these things. She always had to read between the lines when it came to me, and she was always so good at it too.

"You'll tell me, eventually. But I'll let you go and see Lex now. I'll see you in the morning," she says, and then adds, "I love you."

"Love you too, Grandma," I say with a laugh, my face flaming.

I shove my phone back in my pocket and then look over

at the stairwell. I should just leave, forget all of this craziness, but my dick perks back up and I swear it's pointing directly to the door on my right.

Without a second thought, my legs carry me there and my fist is knocking.

I silently make a deal with my dick, that after all the kissing, Lex and I have to have a serious conversation. There are things to discuss, lots of things, like my grandma and the fact that he stole my phone. It's unacceptable.

Fucking inappropriate.

Speaking of inappropriate, my dick is acting like a horny teenager. I hold my suit jacket over my arm, right in front of my crotch. I'm already overheating and my dick is so hard it's straining against my dress pants. It's impossible to hide, and it refuses to be stroked into submission.

I've tried repeatedly, all day. Nothing has made it happy. *Nothing.*

"Why, hello there," a voice says through the ring camera and then the door is flung open, and Lex is standing in front of me, shirtless.

Oh fuck, those tattoos and goddammit, he has nipple piercings.

Of course he does.

And hell, he has a barbell in his belly button too.

I bite back a groan and roll my neck. There's no way I'm making it out of here with my dignity intact.

I shift on my feet, trying to run, but I am locked firmly in place. My body is no longer listening to my brain. My dick has started a coup and my legs, arms, and everything in between have joined the rebellion.

"Come on in. You know, I thought you'd stand me up,"

Lex says, sweeping his arm to the side and I nearly jog into his apartment.

It seems my body doesn't care about consequences. It only wants to feel him pressed against me again.

"Welcome to my awesome abode," he says and my eyes dart around the space.

It's cleaner than I thought it would be. One entire wall is black with bright, colorful tattoo-like paintings adorning it. A large red faux-leather couch sits on the opposite side of the room facing a huge flatscreen. The kitchen is newly remodeled with dark granite counters and a trendy subway-tile backsplash and when I look straight ahead, a small hallway leads to what I assume is the bedroom and bathroom.

"Can I take your coat?" Lex asks as he locks the door behind him.

I shake my head, not wanting to give him any ideas, and if he sees the size of my boner, he will definitely get ideas.

Lex cocks his head and then reaches out and gently moves the suit jacket away.

"Whatcha hiding in there, Willy?" he asks, but he knows already. How can he not see it?

Goddammit, I curse my red hair and pale complexion for giving my embarrassment away. There's no hiding how I feel. My skin displays it openly for all to see.

"You're horny for me, aren't you?" he says, his hand creeping a little closer to my straining dick.

I unintentionally arch my hips toward him. My dick wants what it wants. But Lex evilly snatches his hand back and his eyes twinkle as he watches me.

"Oh, not yet. We'll get to that."

"We won't," I manage to say, even though I'm already panting for it. "I only came here to talk."

Lex raises an eyebrow. "Is that so? It seems your penis disagrees."

I shift on my feet again and Lex reaches out, straightening my collar. Just the feel of his hand on me makes my heart rate skyrocket. I shouldn't let him do that. It's dangerous. I obviously have some sort of heart condition.

"Now you said you wanted to talk, so go ahead. Get it all out so we can move on to the fun stuff."

I clear my throat, my mind scrambling to remember why I'm here.

*Why the fuck am I here?*

*Think, dammit.*

"You stole my phone," I blurt.

"Old news, William. And yes, I did. I was protecting Brenda. It's nothing personal."

"It was personal to me."

Lex's fingers move up to the skin of my neck and my entire body lights up. My blood is lava. My phone is forgotten. I could give two shits about it. Who the fuck needs a phone anyways? Not me.

Keep touching me, Lex.

"William, are you done bemoaning *all of the things* that have happened in your poor life? Can we just move past all of this pretending? I know why you're here. You know why you're here. Everyone knows."

I swallow because he's right. I'm a fucking joke. Who the hell am I kidding? My shoulders slump a little, the last bit of fight leaving me. Okay, dick, you win.

"Thank Zeus. I couldn't stand another minute of your nagging. So, how about we start tonight's lesson with kissing," he says, his voice lined with a hint of excitement. "I'm going to give you some pointers and then we're going to practice for as long as you need until you get it just right. No one flunks my class."

I wet my lips nervously and he bites down on his, eyeing me like a shark circling a wounded seal. I am so screwed.

"Go sit on the couch and I'll be right over."

He walks into the kitchen, and I watch his ass as he goes. It's impossible not to, he's wearing the tightest black jeans I've ever seen and I can't tear my eyes away. I want to do things to his ass. I've never felt the urge to touch an ass before, but fuck I want his. I want to touch it, lick it, bite it, and push my dick inside of it.

Lex reaches up above the sink and opens a cabinet, and I just stare at his toned, tattooed back, as he pulls down a bottle of whiskey.

"Want some?" he asks, shaking the amber liquid in my direction.

I nod because I need something to help me out here. I am so out of my element it's concerning. I should be running away, and yet, I feel glued to his gaudy pleather couch.

"Good. You look like you need it," he says and then saunters back over, handing me a glass half full of whiskey.

"Now, let me clear something up," he says, taking a long-drawn-out sip.

I do the same, feeling the liquid warm my insides as it moves down my throat.

"Just because I'm doing this doesn't mean I'm changing my opinion about you. I still think you're a shit grandson and an overall terrible person, but you taste like candy, and I feel sorry for you."

I take another large gulp. "Anything else?" I ask because this guy doesn't mince words. I hate it and I sort of like it. I always know what he's thinking or feeling. I never have to guess. Growing up the way I did, there was so much guessing with people and I was always sort of shit at reading between the lines. It was exhausting. So Lex is like a breath of fresh air.

He mulls it over and then nods. "And as I've said before, you'll take Brenda away from me over my dead body. She's an important part of my life and I won't be walking away from her. Ever. I'm not stealing money from her. It's insulting that you think that."

Truthfully, I'd eyed her accounts when I'd gotten to the office after brunch. They were intact. I wasn't quite sure if he really was sincere or was playing the long game here. But only time will tell, and right now, I wanted time to move faster so I could get to the good stuff.

We both know the real reason I'm here.

"Okay. Are you done now?" I ask, wanting to just get on with it. I'm squirming.

"Yes. I think I got it all out. Now, lesson one, I'm going to shove my tongue down your throat and you're going to reciprocate."

*Oh, sweet Jesus. Yes, please.*

I throw back the remaining whiskey, feeling slightly buzzed, and turn toward him, my suit jacket still over my crotch. It's not doing a very good job of hiding anything. My dick looks like Mt. Rainier through all that fabric.

Maybe Lex will scale it with his pierced tongue.

Lex sets his half-finished drink down on the table and then saunters toward me, stopping inches away, his flat stomach and light dusting of hair below his belly button on display right in front of my face. His jeans hang low on his narrow hips and it's so damn sexy, my fingers itch to touch him. He grabs onto my jacket and whips it away from me and then smirks when he sees the sizable bulge in my pants.

"Still excited, isn't he?" he says, straddling my thighs and plopping down on my lap, purposefully sliding against my hard length and eliciting a soft moan from me.

"Apparently," I manage to say, my trembling hands curled into fists at my sides

Lex reaches down and grabs onto each of them, bringing them between us. He pries my fingers open and then plants them right on his ass.

"It's nice, isn't it?" he asks, and I flex my fingers to feel him. And yeah, he has a nice ass; it fits perfectly in my hands. "How about we make out for a bit and once you've come in those nicely pressed pants of yours, I'll strip down and you can run your hands all over me?"

I let out a ragged breath.

"I'll let you explore for as long as you want."

*Oh, Jesus.*

"Have you ever touched anyone like this before?" he asks, and I just shake my head.

Lex rests his hands on my shoulders and arches into me and my eyes flutter from the friction on my hypersensitive dick. He drags his fingers slowly up to my face, cupping me softly.

"I am going to be all your firsts, William.

*Fuck, yes, please.*

"But first, let's start with the basics. Nice and slow kissing. Light pressure."

He leans forward and presses his mouth to mine, and I just breathe him in. *Fuuuuck.* He smells good, like tobacco and sage.

My dick is aching, and my balls are drawn up against me. I feel like I'm going to come already, and he's only just brushed his lips against mine.

Wait. Oh shit, now he's sucking and tugging on my bottom lip. That's even worse. I'm whimpering.

Oh, my *fucking god*, his hands are in my hair. I didn't even know my scalp was an erogenous zone, but the way he's pulling on the strands is making my eyes roll back in my head.

It's like I've spent the last thirty years of my life walking around in a bubble and Lex just popped the shit out of it. Now I'm experiencing all these foreign sensations. My skin is oversensitive, and my sense of smell is heightened; I can even hear him more clearly.

The sound of his mouth moving against mine is the sexiest thing I've ever heard. Wet and raw. It sounds like he's sucking on a lollipop.

Lex pulls back and a whine escapes me.

*Don't stop. Feels too good.*

"Hmm. Better. Now, let's go open-mouthed. Touch the tip of your tongue to mine and let me guide you. And, William, don't be afraid to make sounds. Now is not the time to be so quiet. I want to *hear* what I'm doing to you."

I swallow as he tilts his mouth onto mine, and then his tongue is touching mine, sliding against it, and I'm panting into his mouth. I want to be in control, but I'm not. Not with Lex. I'm just helpless and *I like it.*

I groan when he rubs his dick against mine and my hands grasp tighter onto his ass.

He grinds against me, and I am so damn close, I'm going to embarrass myself. Fuck. I am. I'm going to come in my pants.

I've never done that before.

But thankfully, someone up above is watching over me because Lex rips his lips from mine and strokes his thumbs across my cheeks gently.

"Much better. You just needed a little encouragement," he says and then goes back in for seconds. I just let him consume me. He sucks on my tongue and bites down on it, and the sounds I'm making are completely embarrassing, but I'm helpless to do anything but make them. I've completely lost control.

"Yessss, those sounds," Lex purrs, pressing kisses from the corner of my mouth, up my jaw to my ear.

The tip of his tongue slides around the lobe and he bites down on it, causing my entire body to shiver.

"Pleasure points," he whispers in my ear, and then he moves his mouth down to my neck and bites right against my pulse. "There are so many I can show you."

*Oh god yes. Show me all of them. Everyday. Just attach your lips to my skin.*

"More practice first?"

"Mmm," I hum, and he smirks at me. I'd usually be irritated with someone looking so arrogant, but he's so fucking hot that all I can do is lean forward and smash my lips to his. All of my concerns about him fade away in the haze of my lust.

He chuckles a little, but his humor evaporates as he opens his mouth and sucks on my tongue once more.

God, why is that so hot? In theory, it's disgusting, all the germs and spit being exchanged, but in practice, it is making my dick leak. My boxers are completely damp.

He thrusts against me as he fucks into my mouth, and I'm a hot writhing mess beneath him.

I remember in high school when my friends would talk about dry humping and I'd just regarded it as something kind of ridiculous. What was the point?

But now I see all the points. It's mapped out in perfect precision.

Holy shit, this is hot.

Lex thrusts against my cock just right and I feel my orgasm start before I can stop it.

*Oh no. Oh, fuck it all.*

My balls draw up and I explode in my pants. It goes on for ages, my body twitching and spasming beneath him. My whimpers and moans disappearing down Lex's throat.

When euphoria finally recedes, I inhale shakily through my gaping mouth.

Lex leans back, his eyes moving to my crotch and the inevitable wet spot forming.

"That was inhumanly fast."

I gulp down air and feel my entire body heat in embarrassment.

"And *long*. You came for like an entire minute. I'm kind of jealous."

I can't speak, can't even breathe.

"I liked it. I really fucking liked that. I want to do that again," he adds. "But first, you're a mess. Let's clean you up. I assume you didn't bring a change of clothes."

I shake my head and then feel my cheeks flush.

"Told you to, but did you listen? No, you did not. I should make you walk around in your own jizz for the rest of the night, but I'm too kind. Brenda told me so. And you're her grandson so...."

He hops off of me, his hard cock jutting against his pants, and I eye it for much too long. It's long and slender, just like him. I want to touch it and run my hands along it.

I want everything that is Lex, apparently.

"It's impressive, isn't it?" he asks, cupping it and then

extending his hand out to me. I slip my fingers through his as he pulls me up.

At that exact moment, my phone buzzes in my pocket, but I ignore it. I have other things on my mind, more important matters.

Like the fact that Lex is going to strip down naked, and I get to touch his bare skin. I want to trace those tattoos, pluck at the rings in his nipples, and even touch his dick.

I make a mental sign of the cross in my head because heaven help me, I'm not going to survive this.

"You going to answer that?" Lex asks and I shake my head.

"It's no one," I reply, my voice broken and raspy.

He eyes me and then asks, "Is it Brenda? Check it, please."

I pull out my phone and see a slew of messages and an unfamiliar number on the screen but I know exactly who they're from.

Shit.

I shake my head. "No. It's not Grandma."

Fuck, not this again. How did she know I was back in town? I told no one but my grandma.

I don't want to deal with this shit, especially not when Lex is right here, holding my hand and looking like dessert.

I turn my phone off and shove it back into my pocket. I'll figure out how to deal with her later.

Lex is eyeing me suspiciously and I flush crimson again under his stare. How does he manage that? All he has to do is look at me and I burst into color.

"Alright, if you say so. Come on, back here," he says, my hand still wrapped in his. He tugs me down the short hallway and into his bedroom. A queen size bed sits up against the wall and on the opposite end of the room is a large desk with multiple computer screens spanning the entire length of it.

There is a large cabinet next to the desk and I wonder for a moment what's inside.

"Sexy, isn't it?" he says gesturing to his computer set up, but my eyes are locked on him.

*Yeah, he is.*

Lex walks over to a small dresser, opens a drawer, and shuffles through it. He tosses me a pair of grey athletic shorts.

"Here. Go change. Unless you want to be naked for this." His eyes slip down me as he runs a hand over his lips. "Yes, being naked for this wouldn't be a chore. Tell me, do you have freckles *everywhere?*"

I don't answer, just clutch the shorts in my hand and move into the bathroom. It's small and slightly cluttered, with hair products and eyeshadows and...are those lace panties?

Does he wear those? Shit, I want to see that. Why the hell is that so hot?

I lock the door and then my eyes snag on a bottle of cologne. Without thinking, I uncap it and take a whiff. *Oh fuck*, that smell makes my mouth water. It makes my entire body break out in goosebumps.

Everything about this man is pure sex.

Must cease and desist.

Abort. Abort!

I quickly cap it and then pull off my pants and boxers, cleaning myself up as best I can. When I look in the mirror, I note that I look utterly ridiculous. My red hair is a mess, sticking straight up in some places from Lex threading his hands through it, so I comb it back into place, but then I notice how I'm wearing a button-up shirt with a tie and athletic shorts. I don't even match.

Hell, why do I even care what I look like?

I don't know, but I do. I care way too much at the moment.

Quickly, I remove my shirt and tie and opt to just leave my chest bare. It's a nice chest, I think. I work out at the gym a few times a week to feel strong and healthy, not really for looks, but I guess I'm defined in the right places. To be honest, I've never given it much thought until now.

I grab my wallet and keys, shoving them into my pocket so I don't forget them. When I reemerge from the bathroom, all thoughts disappear as I stumble to a stop.

Lex is lying on the bed completely naked, his hard cock pressed against his stomach, and his hands tucked casually behind his head. He has tattoos lining his stomach and legs and my god, he has one on the bottom of his foot.

"Come on over, handsome," he says, his dark eyes watching me approach. "And you *do* have freckles everywhere. Will you let me trace them with my tongue?" he asks.

*Yes, I absolutely will.*

He wets his lips and I shudder in complete and utter lust.

"Oh, and before we begin, I have a little secret. I have piercings in places you can't see right now. So, I suggest you look really hard. Don't want to miss any of them."

I swallow roughly. My throat is dry, parched like the desert. I need more than just a glass of water to quench this thirst inside of me.

I know, deep down, I should be wary of him because he's after me for some nefarious reason. I can just feel it. I shouldn't stay, I should leave before too much happens. But right now, I just don't fucking care.

"Come on," he says as I move toward him. "Straddle me. Take your time. I don't have any other plans tonight."

I crawl up the bed toward him, but I don't straddle him

like he says. No, that would be much too tempting. Instead, I sit down at his side and tentatively reach out, running my finger over his tattooed thigh. It's a wolf, all grey and black shading. It's almost symbolic.

Lex luring me into his apartment, threatening to swallow me whole.

I move my eyes to the other thigh and notice that it's Little Red Riding Hood.

I trace the line of her cloak and his muscles jump and flex under my touch as I peek up at him.

"You *are* the big bad wolf," I mutter.

"All the better to eat you with."

He bites down on his bottom lip, his eyes flashing with desire, and I groan lowly.

My entire hand is splayed across his thigh now and I run it up his leg to his waiting cock and his breath stutters.

Ah, so it's not just me affected by this thing between us. He feels it too. A strange sense of power surges through me as my hand wraps around his long straining dick. It's warm and hard beneath my grip and I clench him a little harder.

His chest heaves, and when I stroke up the length of him, he groans.

"You have soft hands," he mutters. "What lotion do you use? I need to buy some."

I don't answer because my eyes are caught on the two silver barbells right at the base of his penis and I can't breathe.

So much metal on one body. Where else is he hiding these piercings? I need to spend hours exploring him, mapping out the lines of his body.

"That's a pubic piercing," he says, and I run my thumb over it.

His breath hitches and my eyes flash to his. They're hooded and regarding me intently.

"I have more. Like I said, you need to look *really hard* and," he licks his lips, "get really close."

I swallow roughly and release his dick, moving my hand up his stomach and I watch in fascination as the muscles bunch under my fingers.

"Oh, I like that," he says as I move up his chest and swirl my fingertips around his nipples. They pebble under my touch, the barbells through each glimmering in the soft lamp-light of his room.

"Where are the rest?" I ask roughly.

"You have to find them. Like hide and seek. If I tell, it's cheating," he says, and I pull my hands away and lean back on my heels, feeling overly flushed and warm.

Jesus. What would sex be like with him? I'd ignite into a fireball.

"Turn over," I say, and Lex immediately rolls onto his stomach. Oh, I like when he listens. There are tattoos littering his skin on his ass cheek, his legs, and his shoulders.

He's all metal and ink, makeup and chaos.

My hand runs up his calf, the back of his thigh, and then both reach out to knead the swells of his ass.

The ass I can't tear my eyes away from. I want to spread him, touch his hole, taste him.

"Don't be shy," he groans into the pillow as if reading my mind.

I hesitantly spread his cheeks and look. God, he's hairless down there. I slide my thumb against him, and the hole puckers.

I've never even thought about it, but maybe I should get waxed? Trim the bush around my dick. Is this what he finds attractive? Is it how all men are supposed to look? I'm suddenly feeling self-conscious.

Fuck.

Why am I like this?

"You want to slide your fingers inside, don't you?" Lex says, completely oblivious to my internal thoughts. "Go on. I always like ass play." I slide my thumb against him again.

I gulp and debate it momentarily because that would be ridiculously irresponsible. I know he wants more than he's telling me. And I feel like I should care more about why he's doing this with me, but honestly, I don't. I just want to experience this.

Lex leans up and grabs something off his end table and then reaches back and squirts some lube onto my fingers. I stare at them, shiny and wet, and then without thinking, I slide two fingers right inside his tight ass, and he takes them easily.

He shifts onto his knees, his face pressed into the pillow, his arms reaching back, pulling his cheeks apart so I can watch myself tunnel into him.

Hell, it's a sight. It's completely hedonistic.

"God, yes," he mutters when I slide my fingers up as far as they can go.

I crook them a little and he moans. So, I do it again, thrilled that I'm pulling those sounds from him.

"Yes, William, just like that. Scissor them open a little. Yes, oh fuck," he pants.

He arches his back a little more as my eyes rove over his ass, and that's when I see it. I freeze my fingers deep inside of him.

"Oh, you found the guiche piercing," he groans as he peeks over his shoulder. I run my free hand across the barbell right behind his balls and he hisses. He starts to slowly fuck his ass against my hand and more curses fly from his mouth.

"Touch it again," he begs, and my fingers move to grasp onto his balls, my thumb running over the barbells. I roll them in my palm as my fingers drive inside of him, and then one of Lex's hands falls from his ass cheek.

His arm begins to move wildly, and I know what he's doing. I've been doing it so much lately my cock aches. He's jerking his dick as I finger his ass.

Fuck, this is so hot. My dick is throbbing in my shorts. I want to mount him and slide it inside.

I could, too. He'd probably let me.

This is getting so out of control and moving way too fast. I don't really trust him. But, strangely, none of this feels wrong. It feels one hundred percent right.

"Right there. Keep going. There, *there*," he says as I peg something inside of him that makes him cry out.

I suddenly feel his body jerk, his asshole clenching tightly around my fingers as he shudders and comes. I can smell his release as it soaks into the sheets.

My god, the sight of him, the feel of him. My entire body heats as Lex collapses onto the bed, rolling on his side. My fingers reluctantly slip from him and I just stare at where they'd been previously lodged.

"God, that was better than it should have been," he mumbles. "You are a fucking surprise."

He peeks up at me and a small smile pulls his lips up. "You have a way with your fingers," he says, and I blush.

"I need to..." I say, glancing down at my dick pushing out from the fabric of his shorts. "I need to go."

"Or you could stay, and we could practice some more.

There is so much we could do. We could set aside our differences for just a while longer."

But the fog of my lust lifts just enough for me to think clearly. This man wants something from me. I just had my fingers up his ass, his tongue down my throat.

I'm wearing his fucking clothes.

And my ass is not waxed. I'm not ready. I am so not ready.

"I need to leave," I say, stumbling off the bed and knocking into his computer chair.

Lex has turned onto his back, his sexy body on full display and I wrench my eyes away from him. If I look too long, I'll jump on him and stick my dick right up the hole I just stretched.

"Thank you," I manage to say because my grandma didn't raise me to be rude. But the words fall flat between us, and Lex just arches an eyebrow at me.

"So this is how it's going to be?" he asks.

I nod, and then I turn and flee.

It's only when I'm in my car that I realize I'm only wearing athletic shorts and nothing else.

I even left my damn shoes.

# CHAPTER FIVE

## WILLIAM

I lean back in my office chair and stare at the door. Last night has been replaying over and over in my head, and once again, my dick perks up in remembrance despite any and all common sense.

All I have to do is think of him and there it goes. Up, up, up. It's a serious problem. I try to ignore it, but it persists, and I know, *I know* deep down that Lex is doing all of this practicing with some ulterior motive in mind. He doesn't even like me. In fact, all he does is insult me. So he must be trying to distract me from the bigger issue—like how he's possibly stealing from my grandma. Even though I'm not entirely convinced that's the case, I know he wants *something*. I just don't know what it is.

I'm slightly concerned, but at the same time, I'm very intrigued. My dick has grown a mind of its own and its sole focus is Lex. I've learned that I won't get anything done if I don't take care of this right now. I've tried going to the gym—running on the treadmill and lifting weights for several hours straight until I'm utterly exhausted—but it doesn't help. I'm still hard, day and night.

I quickly stand up and lock my office door, my protruding dick almost knocking over a pencil holder on the edge of the desk.

I sigh as I glance down at it. This is becoming burdensome. The dick is unhappy until I stroke it a few times.

When I make it back to my desk, I look at my schedule and pull my cock out, stroking my hard length once and then exhaling deeply.

I have thirty minutes before my next call with a client. In that amount of time, I can get off three times.

I've tried it. Do not recommend. It kind of hurts.

I'm mid-stroke when my cell phone suddenly lights up.

I glance down and see a local number I don't recognize. I shouldn't answer it, because it could be *her,* but I do it anyways.

Because it could be *him.*

My finger punches the green button, and a familiar voice permeates the room.

"What are you doing, William?" Lex says, his voice much too sultry for an afternoon call. My dick twitches in my hand at the sound of his filthy voice. I remember it from last night. The things he said and the way he moaned when my fingers were wedged up his ass.

I stroke my dick faster because I can't help myself. Bad habits and all that.

"Working. What do you need?" I say, proud that my voice comes out entirely even.

"I was just calling for a...friendly chat."

I doubt that very much, but I don't hang up on him. I can't quite seem to push the end-call button.

"Chat about what?"

*God, keep talking. I could come from just listening to you. Talk Lex-isms to me.*

He hums over the phone and my fist continues to work itself over my straining shaft. I went from not being interested in sex to wanting to fuck at all hours. I feel like I'm going crazy. I have pondered making a doctor's appointment to discuss it. What's the opposite of erectile dysfunction? Because I'm pretty sure I have that.

"I wanted to talk to you about a custody agreement," Lex says.

"You're insane." Oh, but in such a good way. I like how weird he is. I'm still concerned about his intentions with my grandma, but mostly I just want to kiss him again.

"And yet, you still want me," he whispers, and my fist tightens on my dick. Because yes, I do. It's obvious. You just need to look at my flushed, overheated skin to know I'm into this guy.

I wet my mouth. "I do not."

He chuckles and then says, "I know what you do when no one else is around. I see and know all, William."

Oh, fuck, the way he says my name. Precum dribbles out of my dick, and I close my eyes as I fuck my fist faster.

"You were such a bad boy last night. You left your clothes at my place when you ran away. You even left your shoes. So, being the good Samaritan I am, I thought I'd stop by later today, drop them off, and we can discuss things. Man to man."

"Fine," I say, my pulse accelerating because I *want* to see him.

"I'll be at your office at three. Cancel clients for me,

William. I want to do things to you in your office," he says, and I bite back a groan as he hangs up.

I slam my phone down, lay my forehead on the desk, and pump myself relentlessly until I come all over the carpet. I need to leave a massive tip for the janitorial service. They don't get paid enough to clean up my mess. It's embarrassing. What they must think of me. I need to have Jason buy some Kleenex so I can come into tissues like a normal human being. Or maybe I'll bring a sock to work and just use that instead.

I cannot continue to shoot my mess everywhere like a geyser.

This is not Yellowstone National Park.

After cleaning myself up and attempting to wipe up the rug, I force myself to focus, but it's torturous. I slog through my workday, crunching numbers and reviewing paperwork. I even take a few phone calls, and it feels a little like a slow murder of my soul. Maybe Lex was right, this place is a morgue. I want to be back in his apartment, running my hands over his warm body, finding those hidden piercings, and running my tongue over his tattoos.

I count down the minutes until he appears and thank fuck he's a little early because I was withering. As soon as I hear his voice in the hallway, my heart rate picks up and I sit straighter in my chair.

Lex strides in, looking sexy as hell with Jason trotting after him, flushed and irritated. So basically, business as usual. I didn't hire Jason for his social skills.

Lex rolls his eyes as he swats the air around him. "Go away, Jason. You and your centipede fingers will never go near me again, or I'll pluck them off one by one," Lex bites out.

Jason looks to me, probably expecting me to take his side, but I just nod to the door and his eyes narrow.

"Seriously?" he asks, and I nod again. Because at this moment in time, I will always choose Lex, despite knowing I probably shouldn't. Jason and his unwavering loyalty don't stand a chance.

He huffs and puffs but still closes the door behind him without a fight, leaving me alone with Lex. Beautiful, sexy, intriguing Lex.

He looks particularly delicious today in grey Converse, purple skinny jeans, and a black tank top.

I should be more conflicted, but I'm not. I just want him.

"Hello there, William," he says with a wide smile as he walks over to me. "Your assistant really needs a health checkup. He's not well. He sweats like a pig."

I lean toward him slightly. "Pigs don't sweat."

"Even more concerning then."

I fold my hands on top of my desk and meet his stare. My dick is already painfully hard in my pants, but I refuse to wiggle around in my seat to help ease the tension. I will sit perfectly still for as long as I can.

My ass moves in the seat.

Jesus fucking Christ.

It just wants out of this chair and onto his lap. It wants to sit on his sexy pierced dick.

"Here you go," he says, setting my clothes down on the desk and then perching on the corner nearest me. "I washed and folded these for you, but full disclosure, I did use them to jack off after you left. Stuck them right over my face as I came. It had to be done. I woke up painfully hard imagining your fingers inside of me and couldn't help myself."

I glance at the fabric, imagining the act he just described, and my skin heats. I should have stayed longer so I could watch him come all over again.

But no. Instead, I ran away and drove home shirtless and shoeless with a raging boner and a strung-out look on my face. Had I been pulled over, the scene would have been straight out of an episode of *Cops*.

"But no matter, here I am," he says as he reaches out, grabs onto my tie, and tugs me toward him. I roll right in between his long legs, my head tilted up toward his.

His lips press against mine without warning and I sigh into it, my hands sliding up his thighs and grabbing onto his hips.

I know I'm no good at this, but hell, I don't really care. I just want to keep tasting him.

My cell phone buzzes on my desk near his leg, but I ignore it, too distracted by his body.

It buzzes again and again, annoying and incessant, so I reach for it, trying to turn it off without wrenching my mouth from his, but Lex is already sidetracked.

Dammit all.

"Who is that?" he asks, and I let out a shaky breath.

I swallow and shake my head. "No one."

And it's not even a lie. She is no one.

"Oh, it's someone," he says as my phone lights up again. "And you're going to tell me, William."

His hand reaches down and massages my dick like it's some kind of magic eight ball that will reveal everything, and it kind of works because I blurt, "I have a stalker...of sorts."

Huh, for some reason I feel less anxious saying that word while he's rubbing my dick.

His hand stills against me.

"A stalker?" he asks gruffly.

"Yes," I say and arch into him, wanting him to keep touching me.

All thoughts of my stalker disappear when he's this close to me.

"Hmm...come over again tonight," Lex says, his fingers flexing around me, and I groan. "We need to get in more practice. There are things I want to do to you."

Oh god, whatever it is, I won't survive it. My dick is going to fall right off from overuse.

He lets go of my aching cock and stands up. Then one of his hands slides through my hair and he tilts my head back so my eyes are forced up to his.

"And of course, the pink elephant in the room...we have this stalker to discuss."

I swallow because of course he wouldn't just let it go. Lex seems like he holds onto things for years.

"Bye, love. See you soon."

———

I amble up the stairs to Lex's apartment, adjusting my boxers, and groaning at the feel of being completely bare down there.

Waxing my balls and asshole had never even crossed my mind up until yesterday. But once I got a good look at Lex naked, I'd obsessed over it until my fingers were flying across my phone and booking a reservation at the Wax Factory after work.

*Good lord*, I did not expect that amount of pain and humiliation from one visit. I'm not sure I'll ever do it again. The lady took one look at the bush around my dick and smirked. She fucking smirked.

Then she said she needed sunglasses from how bright my face turned.

She thoroughly enjoyed humiliating me. I'm convinced

estheticians are just sadists who learned how to turn their proclivities into a profitable business.

When she asked me to bend over and spread my ass cheeks, I nearly died.

But I did it anyways.

Lex better fucking notice that I did this for *him*.

My knuckles rap on the door and when it swings open, I stumble and have to catch myself on the door jamb because Lex is completely naked save for a pair of red lace panties. I immediately recognize them as one of the pairs I saw in his bathroom last night.

I think they're made especially for men because they cup his dick perfectly. It's like he's gift wrapped just for me. I want to unwrap him with my teeth.

"Ah. You like?" Lex asks, grabbing my hand and pulling me inside. I can't even speak, not that I speak often. But right now, I can only gape. I'm a fish.

He spins around and I take in the thong right up his ass crack.

Holy *fuck*.

He chuckles evilly like the supervillain he is, and starts to undress me.

"Best to take all of this off before we practice. We both know what a hair trigger your dick has. I know it is very, very impatient."

He's absolutely right. It's completely unhinged at this point.

When I'm completely nude, my clothes in a pile on the table, Lex glances down and runs his tongue across his teeth.

"My, you are nicely groomed. Looks fresh," he adds, running a hand over the reddened skin near my groin.

"Did they do your ass too?"

I look away, wanting to die of mortification.

"Turn around. Let me see."

I don't move, but he's able to maneuver me to turn, and then he's pressing on my back, bending me over. I don't even fight it. I just bend like the slut I am.

His spreads me open and a low moan escapes his mouth.

"Did you do this for me?"

I refuse to answer. *Refuse*.

"I know you did, William. You might as well admit it," he says as he runs a finger up my crack. My hips buck and I gasp.

But then his hand is suddenly gone and I snap back up, shaking my head. I've never been so embarrassed in my life, and despite it all, I like it. Do I like being humiliated by him? Is that my kink?

Lex pulls his bottom lip between his teeth. "I can read minds and I know you did it for me. So you don't need to admit it out loud. Just know that I know."

God, he's certifiable.

"Come with me," he says, grabbing onto my straining, leaking dick and walking me into his room like a dog. I nip and pant at his heels because he's using my cock as a leash and I'm desperate for whatever lesson he has in store for me.

"I was thinking we should practice some more kissing, and definitely a hand job or two because it's obvious you cannot concentrate right now."

I huff and he smirks at me, slowly caressing my dick, and any remnants of composure I was hanging onto before completely disintegrates. My eyes are rolling back into my head and I'm moaning.

"God, you moan like a whore."

His voice only makes me louder.

"You barely ever talk, but you're fucking loud when you want to be, aren't you, William? You're loud for *me*."

His hand moves faster, and I reach out and grasp onto him, pulling him in for a kiss. It's sloppy and messy, but Lex guides me with his pierced tongue like the expert he is. In a matter of seconds, I'm climaxing violently against him, my come splattering across his hand and stomach and dripping onto the floor.

The kisses slowly stop, and Lex pulls away from me.

"Feel better?" he asks, and I glance down, seeing my mess smeared across his lace panties.

I take a mental picture because it may be the hottest thing I've ever seen. This is going to be jack-off fodder for years to come.

"Yeah," I breathe and Lex smirks at me.

"Good, that's good. Now let me clean up and then we can discuss Brenda."

"Jesus," I mutter, running a hand over my warm face. "Can you at least put on clothes first?"

His eyes narrow with mischief. "Oh, Willy, I will wear whatever I want, and you'll like it."

He returns in just a pair of blue lace panties, and I internally groan. God, he's killing me. I can't even function with him dressed like that. Let alone bargain.

"I can see it in your eyes...you love them. You want to tear them off with your teeth. Hmm, actually, now that I mention it, maybe I'll let you. But first, we need to discuss a few things. I can't let you get me sidetracked."

"Please, put some clothes on," I nearly beg, my body already warming and ready to go again.

He eyes me and he smiles. "Hmm, I'm afraid that won't work in my favor. I'll stay like this, thank you very much."

I sag a little, knowing that I'm going to cave. I'll give him anything he wants in this moment. I've lost millions of brain cells just being in his presence.

"I need to put clothes on first," I say, wanting an extra layer of protection. He's utterly charmed me. I am completely bewitched. But before I can move, Lex suddenly reaches out and grasps onto my throat.

"You'll do no such thing, William. I like looking at you naked."

My dick twitches between my legs at that commanding, slightly psychopathic tone.

"Now, first things first," he says, his hand sliding from my neck down to my chest. "This stalker. Who is it?"

Just thinking about her makes my dick sad. It just hangs limply between my legs, pouting.

"I need a drink first," I mutter.

Lex cocks his head, his finger swirling around the perimeter of my belly button. "Is it really that bad?"

I shrug. That's all relative, isn't it? Is it terrible? No. But is it a nuisance? Absolutely. I could live without the hundreds of text messages she sends me and the phone calls at all hours of the night.

And the pictures.

I shudder.

He hums knowingly as he walks into the kitchen, and my eyes follow his lush, lace-clad ass all the way.

Lex reaches up into that cabinet, his ass cheeks flexing as he does so, and then pours me a drink. Our fingers slide together as I grab it and I bite down on my bottom lip to keep a gasp inside.

I want to be near him, pressed against his body, but I can't. Not yet. I have to behave with some kind of decorum.

So, instead of draping myself across him, I press my lips to the glass he's handed me and sip at the amber liquid. At this rate, I'm going to be an alcoholic and a sex addict by the time he's done with me. I'll need a stint in rehab to recover from this man.

"Now tell me about this stalker. Who is it?" Lex says, pouring himself a glass and leaning his sexy hip against the lip of the counter.

He runs his tongue across the rim of his glass for no apparent reason other than to torment me. I wrench my eyes away.

Must. Not. Look.

"A woman from work. She was one of my assistants. She did payroll, amongst other things."

He arches his hips a little and my eyes are drawn to his dick.

"Tell me more, William. Eyes up here."

My eyes slash to his and god, his face is *everything*. How is he so masculine and yet so *pretty* at the same time? It almost hurts to look at him.

"Uh...she became slightly obsessed with me," I manage to say.

"Ah, I can see that. You have an odd way of endearing yourself to people. I can see someone taking it too far."

Wow, was that an actual compliment he just gave me? And isn't *taking it too far* exactly what we're doing right now?

"I fired her when she became inappropriate, and I thought I had rid myself of her. I changed my number a few times, but she managed to find it again somehow. She was the reason I took the job in Florida. I was trying to get some space."

"You can't escape crazy," he says.

"Seems like it," I mutter.

Lex examines me for a moment, and then asks, "So that's why you left Brenda?"

"Yes. It was a hard decision, but this woman was showing up at my office, constantly coming onto me, and then when I got a restraining order, she just started sending me things and calling all the time. I had to change the restraining order to include texts and messages because it was too much. But it didn't help. She kept breaking the order, but the cops didn't do anything because they couldn't find her. So, I took that contract job for six months hoping that when I came back she would have given up and I could start fresh."

My grandma was the best thing in my life and I hated leaving her, but I was overwhelmed by anxiety and the stress. I'd discussed it with her beforehand, and she told me to go. She practically pushed me onto the plane.

So I left.

Lex's eye twitches slightly as he takes it all in and then he's striding to his laptop on the kitchen counter.

"Alright fine. I need her name, any identifying info, and that number she was calling and texting you from."

I sip on the whiskey some more. "Why?"

"Oh, sweet William, you don't want to know," he says, and I swallow.

"Are you going to hurt her?"

Lex eyes me. "Maybe. If need be."

My god, I shouldn't even be entertaining this, but I end up telling him everything I know. "Susana Beech, age thirty-four, not married, has a pet gerbil."

"A gerbil, really?" Lex asks with a wry laugh.

I shrug and sip more at my whiskey.

"Anything else?"

"I never took the time to really get to know her, but she sure knew me."

I remember the night when I'd snapped and fired her. She cornered me and took off her clothes. I ran away, afraid of how that might look—a male boss and his female employee, the power dynamic between us.

I terminated her employment immediately after that and changed my number.

But I still found her outside of my work, outside of my home.

She was crazy. She *is* crazy.

Shit, maybe I attract crazy people.

"Now give me that number she's been calling you from," he says.

I show him my phone and he scrolls through my messages, his expression darkening with each second that passes.

Yes, I know it's creepy, Lex. I try to avoid looking.

"Is this bitch for real?" he mutters and I just swig my drink in silence.

Because yes, yes she is. Now he knows why I left for months. To try and escape it.

Finally, he just swipes up and then hands me back my phone, leaning forward and typing something into his computer. And there it is, his beautiful ass perched right in front of me. I reach out and trace the thin line of his thong that is stretched across his hip.

He shudders slightly as he looks over his shoulder. "I'll take care of this for you. Don't you worry that pretty head of yours."

I nod, my breath coming out in little pants.

"Thank you."

"You can thank me when she's gone."

I nod, wondering if he will kill her and then wondering why I don't really care. I need to see a doctor for my dick and a psychologist for my brain because I have some concerning issues.

Suddenly, Lex shuts down his laptop and eyes me.

"Now that that's settled, let's discuss Brenda and a custody arrangement."

The shift in topic jars me slightly. I don't want to talk about my grandma while I'm naked.

"I want full custody," he says.

My eyes snap from his lace panties to his face, and I shake my head. "She's my grandma. You can't just keep her away from me."

"Fine," Lex says, looking slightly irritated, but really, is this man insane? I'm not going to stop seeing her just because he has some weird possessive streak. I mean, he can be possessive with me all day long, but not with my grandma. She's been like a mother to me. She raised me when my parents were deemed unfit.

I'm not going to just stop seeing her. Even when I was away from her for six months, we talked nearly every day.

"When I'm with her, you're not to be around. We can call it a ninety-ten split."

"No, no way. I'll see her whenever I want," I say.

Lex's eyes narrow. "Fine, fifty-fifty, and that's final."

"No. Absolutely not. I'll see her when I want, and you can see her when you want. And if our paths cross, then so be it. I can be civil. Can you?"

He leans into me, his cheeks slightly flushed. Why is he so upset about this? I cannot even begin to understand this man.

"William, oh, William, if you want to play hardball with me then no more sexy times until you give me what I want."

God, that's so unfair. Just when I found my sexual desire, he rips it away.

"Why does it matter so much to you?" I ask.

"Because, William, when you're around I'm nothing to her," he mutters, eyeing the floor.

My chest constricts at his words. Is that why he's being so weird about all this? He thinks I've replaced him. God, is he lonely? Does he have no one in his life? For fuck's sake, now I just want to hold him.

"She adores you," I say and Lex's bottom lip trembles slightly.

"Yes, well who doesn't?"

But I can feel it, that small bit of insecurity, and I hate it, hate that look on his face. He should be nothing but fucking confident.

"Lexington," I say softly, pulling his gaze back to me. "I am not going to give up time with my grandma. But you can see her whenever you want. I won't stop you."

He may still want something from her, from *me*, but I'm almost positive now it's not her money. I'm not going to fight him on it anymore.

"You're forcing my hand by not giving me what I want with Brenda," Lex says.

Okay, now he's just being intentionally stubborn, like a kid having a tantrum. But somehow, it's less annoying when he does it.

But standing my ground is just going to force us to be separated.

I'm literally nauseous about it.

I've only known him for a few days but I've already got it bad, and he knows it. He's using it as a bargaining chip.

"We'll see how fair your penis thinks it is at the end of all this." He runs a hand along my half-hard cock just to be mean. "It's going to be sad, William. Very, very sad."

I gasp when he pinches the tip, but I don't get to experience the sensation for too long because suddenly the front door is thrown open and two guys step through.

I scramble behind Lex and peek over his shoulder, my hands on his waist.

Shit. I'm naked in the middle of his apartment and Lex is wearing nothing but skimpy lingerie. It doesn't seem to bother him though. Nope, he seems totally relaxed being scantily clad in front of these two people.

Who are they?

"Oh, hi there, Eminem," Lex says coolly.

"Oh shit, baby Jesus. August, don't look," the brown-haired man with tattoos squeals, slapping a hand over the other handsome man's eyes.

"Oh, he can look. Can't you, August? I know you want to," Lex drawls.

Eminem narrows his eyes at Lex, his tattooed hand still over the other man's eyes. "Do not tempt him. He's mine. And we both know you have more muscles than me. I don't have that many." He glances down at his stomach. "Shit, should I get on that? Do you like how I am, August? Because you've never complained—"

"Em, you're perfect just the way you are," the other man says, his words soft and gentle.

Oh, the way he speaks to him...makes my heart flutter in my chest. No one has ever spoken to me like that. I don't think I'd mind it, actually.

"And besides, seeing Lex naked is something I'd rather not see," August says, his eyes still closed.

"Rude," Lex mutters. "I'm a work of art."

*Yes, yes, he is.*

"August, just keep your eyes closed while I have words with my friend...and I use that term loosely, Lex," Eminem says, shaking his finger at Lex. "You're walking a very thin line."

Lex shrugs, unbothered, and then reaches back to my hip as if to make sure I'm fully behind him, and then asks, "Why are you here?"

Eminem, or Em, replies, "You were blathering on and on about me being neglectful and we made plans to hang, remember?"

Lex arches an eyebrow at him. "That was tomorrow. Not today."

Em glances at August and Lex sighs. "August, I thought you managed his schedule better."

August shrugs. "I didn't know about this until we were on our way over."

Lex mulls that over and then straightens up. "Well, as you can see, I'm in the middle of something important. Say hello, William."

I just blink at them over his shoulder but can't manage to say anything. I'm equal parts mortified and turned on by just being this close to Lex. I can smell him, and feel the body heat emanating from him. I run my lips across the skin of his neck just to taste him.

I need to get my fill since it seems he's cutting me off as soon as I leave.

He trembles a little as my tongue peeks out and draws a line across his shoulder blade.

"Oh, hello there, William," the tattooed man says and my tongue slips back into my mouth as I'm jolted back to reality. I have to keep it together. We have company. And I'm still naked, licking Lex like an animal.

"I'm Emery, Lex's best friend. And let me tell you, Lex never has visitors. He has a rule about it, actually. You must be *very special*."

Lex stiffens a bit against me. "Shut up, Eminem."

"I don't think I will. You're parading your penis in front of my boyfriend in that sexy underwear. So, this is revenge. Where did you get that, by the way? I think August would like it if I bought some. Babe, without looking at them, don't you think I'd look good in those?"

August just blindly nods.

Lex sighs, and says, "Wow, you suck at revenge. You always get sidetracked and never follow through. And I'll send you the link. Order a size medium."

"Why thank you, and do not use my ADHD against me. You know it's just how I am," Emery replies and then tugs August toward the door. "I'll see you tomorrow, Lex. Nice to meet you, William!"

Lex chuckles a little, but it's cut off abruptly when Emery blurts. "Oh, and just so you know, Lex has cameras everywhere. Beware!"

Lex grumbles under his breath as my eyes suddenly dart all around the apartment.

The door snicks shut behind us and I stumble out from behind him, my hands covering my crotch.

"Is that true?" I ask, feeling equal parts infuriated and turned on. Why is it that the thought of Susana watching me is revolting, but with Lex, it's...something else entirely?

"Oh, don't mind him," Lex says, waving his hand around in the space between us. "I'm just...security minded."

"Did you record this...did you record *everything?*"

Lex's eye twitches again and my cheeks flame.

"Oh," I say and scramble back toward the bedroom, rushing to put my clothes on.

Despite my mortification, my dick is still hard which makes it difficult to pull my pants up. Damn thing. It's always in the way now. It's like I'm walking around all day with a rolling pin in my pants. I liked it better when it was flaccid and obedient.

"You don't have to make this a big deal," Lex says, leaning against the doorframe to the room and watching me frantically dress. "I'm not going to share it. It's for my consumption only."

God, I hate that I like that. That he's going to watch me.

I have deep-seated psychological issues.

"Are you watching me in my...office?" The things he must have seen.

The way his eye twitches makes me realize he has. That's why he called the other day when I was in the middle of fucking myself into oblivion. When he said he knew and saw all, he meant it literally.

"Delete it. Delete it all," I mutter as I pull my shirt on and try to move past him, but he and his sexy panties stop me.

"I won't be deleting it. I'm keeping it. And I'm going to watch it, William, over and over. You are still absolutely delicious, despite being secretly villainous."

He fists my shirt, pulling me into him.

His lips slam into mine, hard and demanding. I should be pushing him away, should be fighting this because I'm angry, dammit, but instead, I just lean into him and let him devour my mouth until I'm weak in the knees.

When he slowly pulls away, I just blink at him dumbly.

His thumb traces the line of my jaw. "Fuck. You taste like candy."

He steps away, and I quickly move past him, my heart thundering in my chest.

This ends now. No more. It's good that he's cutting me off.

He's a psychopath.

God, why does that turn me on even more?

# CHAPTER SIX

## LEX

"Brenda, stop fiddling with that," I say, gently grabbing her cell phone. She has absolutely no regard for it. She used it as a bookmark for her *Star* tabloid magazine the other day. "I'll be back tomorrow and we're going for a walk in the mall. We can get lunch while we're there too."

It's too damn hot to go outside and I don't need Brenda to faint from heat exhaustion. Just walking her to the car in this weather gives me a heart attack. Sometimes she walks ultra-slow too, causing my blood pressure to soar. I think she does it on purpose just to mess with me, the little scoundrel.

"You should see if Martha and Vikki want to come with us. They need to get out as well," Brenda says with a yawn.

Why does she look so tired today? She was fine yesterday. I need to give her more green tea, and hopefully, the exercise tomorrow will boost her energy levels.

I try to put my worries aside and focus on other things.

Like her grandson.

Kinky, insanely delicious William who still hasn't contacted me. It's been two whole torturous days and I'm finding it hard to keep myself away from him. I did send him a little present though, and I wonder if he's wearing them right now.

I've spent way too many hours in front of my computer, watching him in his office, trying to see any hint of my gift on him. But he never pulls his pants down for me to see.

He's unintentionally teasing me and it's driving me crazy.

For one moment, *just one,* I wonder if I'm like Susana, that crazy stalking bitch, but I quickly decide that I'm not.

No, I'd never actually hurt him and William likes me watching him.

I know it for a fact because every day, he locks his office door, sits at his desk, and then his arm moves frantically beneath his desk. Sometimes it's multiple times a day.

He's getting off.

Is he thinking of me while he does it?

He never looked very hard for my tiny camera, despite knowing it's there. I have a sneaking suspicion he's performing for me, even though I can't see much. I should slink in there one night and put a camera under his desk.

I'd like to watch him explode.

"How are things with you and William?" Brenda asks and I direct my attention toward her.

Hmm, I should probably not be having all these filthy thoughts in the presence of his grandmother.

I take her hand and squeeze it gently. Her skin is so wrinkly and soft and it reminds me once more how old she is.

"There's nothing between William and me."

"That's not what he said."

My eyebrows shoot up and I lean a little closer, intrigued.

"Do tell, Bren. Don't keep secrets from me."

She smirks and pretends to zip her lips. Oh, what a monster. She's liking this a little too much.

"Bren," I warn, but she just waggles her eyebrows.

"I'll tell you one thing," she says, holding up an arthritic finger. "He blushed a lot when he talked about you. I've never seen him like that."

Why, yes, he does blush a lot. I love watching all that fair, freckled skin turning the most delicious color pink.

I'm regretting my decision to withhold sex until he's given me what I want because he is so very tempting.

If I concentrate hard enough, I can still taste him on my tongue.

You know, now that I've had some time apart from him and really put some thought into it, I wonder why I can't have both Brenda *and* William. The custody agreement was a little unreasonable, I admit. We can share her, like he said.

I don't like keeping myself from things I want, and I *want* him.

Maybe I'll make a stop by his work on the way out of here, just to check on the state of things. He does have a stalker, after all, which could possibly harm Brenda. It's within the realm of possibility. Yes, it's Brenda that I'm protecting, not William. Not really. This has nothing to do with me seeing those nasty text messages she sent him and feeling the sudden urge to claw her eyes out.

Brenda is my priority and that's why I have to take certain preventative measures.

My phone vibrates in my pocket, and I pull it out to check the screen.

**Diablo:** That bitch was hard to find. Now you owe me double for working miracles. You know what I want.

I smirk down at my phone. I knew he'd come through, and the price was a total steal.

**Me:** Don't worry, you'll get it.
**Diablo:** Should only take you about three hours.
**Me:** Oh, I can do it in an hour and a half. You know how good I am.
**Diablo:** Don't brag. We know your skills are unmatched. Just hurry up. I need it.

Jesus, Diablo is a greedy, impatient fucker. He needs someone to spank him into submission, make him beg a little, and help him shut that smart mouth of his.

I snort at the image.

It would have to be a very special man to accomplish that.

Diablo may be small, but he's terrifying. And so is his family.

All sociopaths, if you ask me.

I shudder at the thought and then peek over and at Brenda. She's asleep—just snoozing all the fucking time.

I'll talk to William about her health when I stop by. We need to come up with a plan. And to be honest, I'd much rather do this with him than fight him on it.

I want to be a team...of sorts.

Yes, a team would be nice.

I tuck a blanket around Brenda's slumbering body and then quietly make my way out of the room. As I'm walking out of the automatic doors, I hear a familiar voice.

"Lex?"

I turn to see a handsome man, leaning against the front desk.

Ah, I vaguely remember him. I met him the other day with his son.

His name, not so much.

I think it starts with an M?

"Hello there," I say, making my way over to him. Behind the counter, Ben watches me approach with wide eyes, his cheeks flushing the closer I get.

I need to nip that little crush in the bud. Just chop it right off.

I have William now.

For the moment, at least.

Well, not at all at the moment actually because I stubbornly cut him off.

I need to fix that *immediately*.

Two days without touching him has proven harder for me than expected. I blame the way he tastes. No one has any right to smell and taste that sweet. I told you he's dangerous—like a Venus flytrap, I'm ensnared.

"You checking in?" I ask the man whose name I can't remember as I send Ben a wink.

Ah, yes, nipping the buds. I need to *remember* to stop flirting with him. Flirting is a bit habitual at this point. I flirt like I breathe.

I don't even realize I'm doing it.

"I am," the man says, smiling widely. "Ben has been so helpful."

I glance over at Ben and smirk when I see his face flame again. Ah, maybe the two of them can get together and have a little fun.

They'd have nice, boring sex.

It would be nothing like what William and I have.

"Well, have fun," I say, wagging my fingers at him.

But before I can leave, the man stops me. "I'm Colin, by the way, just in case you forgot."

"I would *never* forget," I lie and then throw him a saucy smile. "Colin, I believe I have your number."

"And you've yet to use it."

"I have been a bit...*preoccupied*," I say and peek over at Ben who is watching me carefully. Hopefully, he gets the hint. I don't want to hurt his precious soul. He's too innocent for someone like me.

In fact, so is William. But the difference is, I can tell William wants to be corrupted. I see how his eyes light up when I say and do naughty and depraved things. My dick twitches in my pants just thinking about my sexy cum-filled donut. I need to see him, soon. Now, preferably.

"Well, it was nice to see you," Colin says. "I have to take my grandma to the doctor."

"Well, isn't that exciting. I'll try to remember to text."

I won't text. I'm not interested.

Colin sends me a wave and I return it before loping out of the senior living facility.

Just one more job before I can head over to see William.

My phone buzzes and I glance down at it.

**Diablo:** Here's her info.

Oh, Susana, you tried to be sly, but you stand no chance against me. Well, against Diablo. Sometimes I like to delegate. I'd rather be spending my time watching William.

Plus, Diablo works faster than me.

He has a special talent, and we have a barter agreement.

**Diablo:** I can take care of her for you but it's gonna cost.

I ponder that. But realize it will be too much fun to miss, watching this woman squirm. I want her to know that we mean business. Plus, I have a sick desire to meet this vile woman.

**Me:** Why don't we do it together?
**Diablo:** Fine. But you clean up any mess. Just send me the date and time. I'll be there.

Lazy, cheap ass. He always wants to go along for the fun but refuses to do any of the maintenance that goes along with it.

I rush through my next job just so I can get to William faster.

As I park outside his building, I hope he's in his office. I pull up the video feed of him on my phone to check, and sure enough, he's staring right at the camera, his bottom lip pulled between his teeth.

Dirty, filthy man.

He better be wearing those panties I sent him.

———

Jason glowers at me as I make my way toward William's office door. Thankfully this time he doesn't bother stopping me.

Perhaps it was the threat of chopping off those chubby fingers of his. He's still sweating profusely. He has a miniature fan buzzing away on his desk. It's obviously not helping.

"See a doctor, Jason. It's becoming serious," I say as I pass him.

Jason just grunts.

One day I'll show up and he'll be face down on his desk. Deceased.

I won't even be surprised.

I push the door open to see William looking absolutely edible in his chair, wearing a fitted navy suit and silver tie. His hair looks like he's been running his fingers through it and his lips are red and plump from biting them. He looks nothing like a dull and stuffy accountant should look. No, he somehow makes a two-piece suit look purely vulgar.

He glances up at my intrusion and when his blue eyes meet mine, my heart rate triples and my palms sweat.

Hmm, I should speak with Elliot about this and see if it's normal. Maybe I caught Jason's sweaty-man heart disease.

"Look forward to working with you, William," the voice on the speakerphone says and when I wet my lips and eye him, he blushes deeply.

Oh, he's thinking of all the filthy things I can do to him. I'm sure he's missed me. He's just as insatiable as I am.

He ends the call and then stands up abruptly, his chair rolling back and knocking against the wall.

"Who was that?" I ask, closing the door behind me and locking it.

It's just a precaution. I don't want Jason to see anything inappropriate and have a stroke because I'm about to do some very naughty things to William and his virgin dick.

"No one."

"You do realize, I can find out everything about him? I have my ways."

His eyes shoot right up to where my camera is hidden— ah, so he does know where it is—and then he narrows them on me. But it's all a farce. He's not angry with me for spying.

No, the way his erection is pressing out from his pants tells me that he's very excited about the fact that I watch him in my free time.

"I'm hiring a private investigator," he blurts.

"Oh, are you now? How...titillating."

"Yes."

I run a thumb across my bottom lip. "And let me guess... you're going to ask them to investigate *me*. Because you don't trust me? Really, William, don't be so predictable. It's boring."

William swallows, his breath stuttering out of him. God, he sounds like he's having sex and all he's doing is standing there.

This raw attraction I have to him is irrational. I've never felt anything like this. Why did it have to be Brenda's fucking grandson? Did she will this into existence? Because she's been pushing this hard.

"Yes."

I roll my lips between my teeth and then move toward him because, let's be honest, he's too far away. I want to suck his dick. I want to gag on it.

"I can give you all the information you want to know. It'll save you a bundle in fees."

He inhales sharply as I stop just a few inches away.

"You're not going to give me everything I want."

"Oh, but I am," I whisper, reaching out and running my finger along the throbbing vein in his neck. "I'll give you exactly what you need."

"Jesus," he breathes, his eyelids fluttering.

"Yes, worship me, William. Get on your knees and open that pretty mouth."

His eyelids close tightly as he tries to stay in control, but I don't want him in control. I want him writhing.

"But you told me no more of this," he nearly whimpers.

"I changed my mind. I'm very much reformed now."

I slide my finger up across his lips and press it inside his warm mouth and over his tongue. He sucks on it instinctively and moans.

God, this man, why is he so fucking sexy? He's nothing like what I'm used to. He's so reserved and quiet...and secretly freaky.

Suddenly, his desk phone rings, and he glances at it, my finger still in his mouth, his lips suckling on it lightly.

"Go ahead. Answer it," I say, pulling away from his mouth.

He hesitates for just a moment and then leans over and presses a button. A dismal voice sounds from the other end and William starts to answer questions, but I'm not paying any attention to what they're saying. I'm pressing up against him, smelling him.

God, how is it that every time I'm near him he smells even more delicious? Like taffy. Like motherfucking dessert. One day I'm going to smear him in chocolate pudding and lick every delectable inch of him.

He'd let me too. He'd just pant and whine like a good boy.

I run a hand down his silver tie and stop when I hit the belt of his pants.

His skin pinkens and he clears his throat.

Hmm, so he's nervous.

I love this about him.

Slowly, I undo his belt and when the metal clinks open, my fingers move straight to the button of his nice dress pants.

The man on the other end of the phone is droning on and on, and William is answering his questions as best he can while I leisurely remove his pants.

Much to my dismay, he's not wearing the lace panties I'd sent him.

I meet his gaze as my hand traces his boxers and he lets out a quiet huff.

I can see I'm going to have to incentivize him to wear them for me.

They'd match his skin tone perfectly. The woman at the check-out counter told me so.

I reach down and squeeze his hard cock and his eyes roll back in his head.

I love how responsive he is. I've never been with someone so needy before.

I fall to my knees and silently tug his boxers down his thighs. His cock pops out, all flushed reddish-purple and angry.

*Why, hello there.*

My tongue slides seductively across the underside of him and he exhales shakily.

He looks so put-together and professional but I'm on my knees about to take him apart completely until he's sloppy, messy, and utterly wrecked.

Without hesitation, I pop the head of his dick into my mouth and slide it to the back of my throat, letting my tongue ring do what it does best.

I'm going to brag for a moment, so bear with me. I am fabulous at giving head. I've been told so by many. I give it so good, I actually won an award once. I'd made it myself, but still. It counts.

When he hits the back of my throat, I swallow around him, and he grabs onto my head, his fingertips digging sharply into my scalp.

William is still trying to answer the man's questions on the line, something about numbers and deadlines, but he's panting, stuttering, and tripping over his words. I am sucking his brain out through his cock and he can't even answer in English.

I'm pretty sure I just heard a few words in German.

I slide my tongue back and forth on the underside of his cock, popping off of him briefly and then going back in for seconds, and shit, he tastes good down here too. This is getting a little ridiculous. How can someone be so tasty? He's not human, I'm convinced.

I grab his hips, yanking on him and fucking him into my mouth roughly. He thrusts erratically while trying to remain as quiet as possible. He's clutching my hair for dear life, trembling under my touch, absolutely shaking. Every inch of his skin is bright red.

He's going to combust and I'm going to be the reason.

Only me.

I'm so glad I changed my mind about having him.

I'm not going to play hard to get with this man anymore. There will be no fasting. I don't have the self-control. As it is, my dick is painfully struggling to escape my jeans.

It wants out. It wants to play.

The sight of William coming undone is so hot, I could come just like this.

I slide one hand down past his balls and finger his taint. He gasps mid-sentence. The poor guy on the other end of the line must think he's having a seizure.

God, I can't wait to fuck him for the first time.

I'm going to record it so I can replay it and watch that ass stretch out for me while he writhes and whimpers underneath me.

"Hello?" the man says, but William just ignores him. He's quietly quitting. He's done.

I've convinced him that I'm the priority.

Motherfucking me.

His lips part and he's panting and whimpering as I swallow him down my throat.

Blessedly, the call clicks off, and William groans loudly as he unloads into my mouth.

I drink down every last drop before licking him clean.

"Lexington," he mutters, and my god, my name on his lips sounds like a dirty plea.

I swipe at my mouth with the back of my hand and then slowly stand up on shaking legs.

My hand wraps around his tie and I tug him toward me, pressing my lips to his. My tongue slips into his mouth and I let him taste himself on me.

When I finally pull away, I'm breathing heavily, and William's dick is half-hard against his thigh.

"Are you almost done for the day?"

"Yeah."

"Good. Finish up and then let's grab something to eat. We can go to my place after, and you can eat me for dessert." I eye him and then tug on his tie again, just for fun. Who would have thought I'd like a man in a suit this much?

I want to tear off that tie and wrap it around his wrists, around his throat, around his dick.

I started this little sexual exploration with William as a means to exploit him, but now I just want to enjoy him.

"Plan on staying over. I want to do things to you in the middle of the night. Filthy things."

Never have I ever let anyone but Emery sleep in my bed.

But since I'm all of William's firsts, it's only fair that I give him some of mine.

Not that he needs to know this.

"I shouldn't," he protests.

I lean into him, and his chest expands.

"Oh, you should. And you *will*. Now finish up so we can go. I'm hungry. And I'm a cranky bitch when I don't eat."

I take a step back and then lower myself into a chair on the other side of the desk. I throw my legs over the arm and pull out my phone.

I might as well look up this stalker while I'm just lounging here. I need to plan out exactly what I'm going to do with her when I find her. Diablo has already sent me some very gruesome and explicit ways to dispose of her.

I'd prefer not to use lye, Diablo. Thank you very much.

Federal prison would not be a good look on me. Orange is not my color.

But death certificates? Now, those I can do.

Oh, yes, this bitch is going to be very, very dead...on paper.

I can feel William's eyes on me, so I flick mine up to meet his.

"Yes?"

He clears his throat but doesn't say anything. Ah, my silent William, always thinking but never actually speaking. I want to crawl inside his head and listen.

"Carry on, love. I'll wait," I say, and then throw him a sassy wink.

He swallows and pulls his pants up, buckling his belt. Then he sits in his large leather seat, like some kind of king.

I'll gladly be his servant.

I imagine doing dirty things with that calculator.

I can get quite creative.

He fiddles around with his keyboard and speaks to Jason over the phone for a minute and then he's standing up.

"Ready."

"Oh, so am I. So am I."

# CHAPTER SEVEN



## WILLIAM

*I cannot believe he talked me into this.*

I sigh. Yes, yes, I can actually believe it. I am *weak* when it comes to him, and the things he does with his lips and tongue.

When he'd swallowed me down his throat, his tongue ring grinding against my length, I'd nearly passed out while I was on the phone with a very important client.

I'm going to lose business because of this man.

He's going to be the end of me.

But there is no way I am going to be able to get on with my life without him in it. The past two days have been torture.

My only saving grace is the fact that I knew he was watching.

It was total foreplay for me. I'd sit at my desk and jack off to thoughts of him in his room, enjoying the show.

I am a sick, perverted man, and I've made peace with it.

When I finish with work, Lex follows me to my apartment so I can grab a change of clothes. As much as I know I shouldn't spend the night with him, I'm going to do it anyways. He's temptation personified. I'm defenseless against it.

"Your apartment is not what I expected," Lex says, driving me across town to his place.

He'd convinced me to leave my car parked in the garage by kissing me senseless. I just nodded and followed him blindly to his car.

"I'm a simple guy."

"You are not at all what I expected."

I eye him and shift in my seat. The car smells like him, tobacco and sage with a hint of sweetness, and I'm a little heady from it.

"What did you expect?" I ask, so very curious.

Lex grips the steering wheel with one hand and looks over at me.

"I don't know, but I didn't expect a virgin accountant who lives in squalor."

My eyebrows meet. "I don't live in squalor."

"That apartment was shady, William, and I'm the mother-fucking shade. I know these things."

"Well, it works fine for what I need."

It's true, I really am simple. Why do you think I could just pick up and move across the country? It's because I don't have much and I'm okay with that. I'm a minimalist at heart. I packed a few boxes and was good to go. It was a harder move for Jason.

Lex eyes me for a moment and then moves them back to the road.

"We'll see. I should set up some cameras there to make sure you're safe. The guard at the front door was high as a fucking kite. He's more likely to shoot you than an actual intruder."

"I think you watch me enough," I say, and Lex reaches over and sets his hand on my thigh.

"Oh, I could watch you *all day*. And don't pretend like your dick isn't hard right now just thinking about it."

It is. There's no hiding it.

It's reaching up toward Lex, panting.

When he pulls up to his apartment building and we exit the car, he grabs my bag and then reaches over and links his hand with mine.

I've never held another man's hand before. I like it. I think I want to do it all the time.

He pulls me into the elevator and before the doors even close, his mouth is on mine, and I just melt into him.

"You're getting better at this," he says as the bell dings and the doors open.

I blush red at his praise because it seems that's all I can do around him these days. I just pant and flush crimson.

Lex tosses my bag onto his bed and then turns to me. "Well, before we do anything else, I have something for you," he says, his brow furrowed.

He holds out his hand and opens his fingers, and on his palm lies a flash drive.

"For you," he says.

I touch it gingerly and meet his gaze.

"On that is everything you *need* to know about me," he explains and my heart begins to gallop.

"You just have this lying around?" I ask, confused as to

why someone would just have this compiled. Does he give this to everyone he sleeps with?

Or is it just me?

I don't like thinking that it's not just me.

"Of course. I'm always prepared."

I take it from him and slide it into my pants pocket. I'll look at it later. Maybe.

Right now, there are more urgent matters at hand, like the fact that Lex's shirt is riding up his stomach as he pulls the whiskey down from the cabinet.

"Want some?" he asks me.

I nod and he pours me a glass.

I sip at it as he pours himself one and says, "Now before you get on your knees and I teach you how to suck my dick, we need to discuss Brenda."

My eyebrows meet because I do not enjoy hearing those two issues squished together into the same sentence. Sucking dick and my grandma are two very separate subjects and thinking about them at the same time makes me want to gouge my eyeballs out.

"Please warn me before you decide to work my grandma into our sex conversations. But, what about her?" I ask.

"She's sleeping too much."

I sip my drink for a second and then say, "She's old, Lex. It happens."

"She's not that old. She can live another thirty years."

"Lex..."

He holds up a finger. "Do not discount me and my feelings. She's sleeping too much, William."

My heart sinks a little at the distress on his face. Okay, yeah, I get it. He loves her. This isn't about the money. He's just found a sense of belonging. I saw the look on his face, how his lip trembled when he thought she'd replace him with me.

"She's okay. She has a doctor's appointment this week," I tell him.

"Yes, well, fine, but I don't like it. I'd like to attend the appointment," he says, looking distraught when I don't say anything. "Please let me come, William. Please?"

I reach out and link my hand with his, a zing moving through my skin. "You can. Of course you can."

His shoulders slump and he exhales shakily. "Thank you. I didn't want to have to fight you. As tasty as you are, I hate that you're here, taking away my freedom to do as I please."

"You can always help with my grandma. I never made it an issue. You did."

He glances up at me, his eyes wide with realization.

God, this is the most vulnerable I've ever seen him. Not that I've seen much of him. He lives mostly in my dreams and fantasies.

In this moment, though, he seems very sincere.

He cares about my grandma. Who wouldn't? She's an angel. She's gone and adopted this man, and he seems entirely resistant to let her go.

He's also been good for her. I could tell then while talking on the phone with her while I was away. I can tell now with how she lights up when he's around. He's mistaken if he thinks he's so easily replaceable.

I'll have to show him, to remind him that he isn't.

"I'll text you the time and date," I offer.

"I'll be there," he says so quickly that he cuts me off.

He takes a large gulp of his drink and then sets it down on the counter. His head is bent low, his hands clenching the cup.

He takes a deep breath and blows it out, and then it's like none of it happened.

"Good, now that that's done," he begins, his head tilting and his eyes meeting mine, "tell me why you aren't wearing those panties I sent you."

My cheeks heat as I choke on the whiskey. Hell, I'd gotten those deposited on my desk while at work and then had proceeded to do filthy things to them. They're hidden at the bottom of my hamper. They're coated with my transgressions.

"I received them," I manage to huff out.

"Yes, but why aren't you *wearing* them?"

I press the cool glass to my cheek and blink at him.

"Oh. *Ooh*. William," he says, standing up. "You naughty boy. Lucky for you, I bought you extra. Come. Put a pair on and then we can have some fun."

I gulp down the rest of my drink and helplessly follow him into his room. His computer is on and suddenly, I remember.

The cameras. He's recording all of this.

I hesitate for just a second before letting him tug my tie off.

"Hmm," he hums as he begins to unbutton my shirt. My body is positively on fire as he runs his hands across my skin, his glossy black nails in such contrast to my pale, freckled skin. "I want to hate you, but I can't help but want you."

My shirt flutters to the ground and I groan as his hands work open my pants.

"I am dying to see you on your knees, my dick stretching your mouth wide open. I am going to teach you so much."

My pants hit the floor with a clink. I step out of them, and then Lex is sliding his hands into my boxers, slipping them down over my sensitive skin.

When I'm completely naked he moves to his dresser and

plucks something off the top.

"Blue. Your color. They match those pretty eyes," he says, holding out a pair of lacy panties for me to try on. "Go on. Put them on. I want to see."

I gulp and take them from his hand, slowly putting them on, aware that he's watching me and that his cameras are recording this.

It only makes me harder. I guess I can add exhibitionism to my new list of kinks.

When the lace panties are over my straining dick, Lex's tongue pokes out, running over his top lip.

"Perfection. Now...on your knees, pretty please."

I do as he says, sinking to the floor, and I clutch onto his thighs, eager and desperate to taste him. I've been thinking about this all day. All week. Even in my dreams, I devour him. I wanted to do this the minute I stepped through the apartment door, but he'd gotten sidetracked with other things.

I'm so worked up, I'm drooling for it.

Lex undoes his jeans, his cock jutting out, and without hesitation, I suck him into my mouth.

A gasp resonates around the room, followed by a groan because I am lapping and slurping on his dick, ravenous for it. I don't know what I'm doing.

All I know is that I fucking love it.

"Jesus Christ," he pants as I pull him into the back of my throat, gagging myself on him, and then I do it again because I like it.

"Holy fuck," Lex cries out as I gurgle around him. My spit is everywhere, I'm drooling like a leaky faucet, and my eyes are wet with tears streaming out of them. The noises my throat is making are offensive, but I can't stop. I don't want to stop.

I want to consume him.

Lex's hands tighten in my hair as he guides me, fucking into my mouth with precise rhythmic thrusts, and I moan around him, my cock straining against the thin lace trying to contain it. It's going to burst through.

God, I need to come. I want to come.

I reach down and pull myself out, jacking off to the feel of him inside of my throat and the taste of him.

"Goddamn you," Lex moans and wraps his hand around my neck as I gag on him again. "*God. Damn. you.*"

He pounds into my throat and then without warning, he's releasing in my mouth. His warm liquid hits the back of my tongue and I swallow down most of it, the rest slipping down my chin as I frantically unload onto the floor.

When the spasms finally slow, my forehead rests against his thigh while he pets my hair gently.

"That was..." he lets out a shaky exhale, his hands trembling slightly. "What you lack in skill you make up for in enthusiasm."

I peer up at him and our eyes lock. His pupils are still blown out and his cheeks flushed from the orgasm.

I did that.

I feel completely sated and proud at the same time.

"Let's clean up and then do you want to see what you look like on your knees for me, sucking me off?"

The thought of it makes my entire body shudder and I give him a small nod.

"Come on then," he says, helping me to my feet and guiding me to the bathroom where he gently cleans up the mess we made. His hands are so gentle, so comforting, and I just lean into him the entire time.

He leads me back into the bedroom, still completely

naked, and pulls me onto his lap in front of his computer. He opens up the feed of me sliding the panties on as I press back against him.

My god, look at me, all wanton and eager to do whatever Lex asks.

Even the cameras know how gone I am for this guy.

"This is on a secure drive; you don't have to worry about anyone seeing this," Lex says, thinking the stiffness in my body is from concern over this getting out.

The truth is, I'm not really that worried about any of that. Even though I know I should be. But I'm much more focused on the fact that Lex's hand is sliding across my stomach, his breath against my shoulder as we watch me drop to my knees on the screen.

Oh god, I look gluttonous.

"Look at you," he says, shifting beneath me.

I relax a little against him and his hand cups my soft dick, fondling it gently.

Why I'm letting him do this to me boggles my mind, but like hell I'm moving. I want his hands on me all the time.

"That was by far the best blow job I've ever had," Lex says.

I turn my head to look at him and he smirks.

"Shocking, I know."

I return my gaze to the screen and focus closely on Lex who is gasping and grinding into me. He wasn't kidding. He looks unhinged. His head is thrown back, his fingers sinking into my scalp, his lips parted in ecstasy.

I can't believe I had that much of an effect on him.

When the screen goes blank, Lex rests his forehead against my back and presses a kiss to my overheated skin. His hand is still on my dick, cupping it almost possessively.

"How about we watch a movie in bed and then we can go

to sleep?" he says softly.

"Yes, but first," I say, my mind in a slight fog. "Tell me something no one else knows," I manage to get out. I want to know more about this man. I want to know everything he's willing to give me.

Lex freezes behind me.

"You have the flash drive."

"Something that's not on there. Something only you know. Something sacred."

He rolls my balls in his hand, his other hand sliding across my chest. I'm all nerves and sensations. I wonder if I shouldn't have asked this, but it's too late to take it back now. The words hang between us for a long moment.

"Fine." He pauses for a second and then says, "I had a brother. He died when I was ten."

I turn to look at him, my lips brushing against his cheek.

"Lexington," I whisper, feeling my chest constrict, and he presses his lips to my neck.

"That's all you get from me."

I sigh. I'll look at that flash drive later and try to figure out who Lex is.

Maybe.

Honestly, I'd rather he told me, though. Maybe I can get him to spill his secrets, one by one.

I stand up and Lex moves into bed. I lay between his spread legs, just resting my head against his shoulder as he pulls the blanket up over us and turns on the TV.

His steady breathing is soothing and I feel myself relax even further. I don't quite understand how I know so little about him and yet, I feel so comfortable with him. How can he possibly be everything I need all at once?

"I don't have siblings," I tell him, my eyes closing. "I was an only child."

Lex inhales but doesn't release it, he just sits completely still behind me, holding his breath.

"Brenda became my legal guardian when I was twelve."

He exhales a little, his hand slipping into mine, our fingers interlocking.

"Why?" he asks softly. "There has to be a reason."

"My parents were...awful."

Well, that is another word for it, but I don't tell him more than that. I will, just not now.

"You're lucky you had Brenda."

"I am. She loved me when no one else did."

Lex slides his hands up my chest. "Do you love her, William?"

"How could I not?"

"Yeah, I know. I so fucking know."

We're silent for a while, the movie playing in the background, his hands moving up and down my skin tenderly. I can practically hear his mind churning. It's always moving, always plotting.

What does he want from me right now?

"I had no one," he replies suddenly, his words just whisps of letters and syllables.

I squeeze his hands against mine because I know. I fucking *know*.

We're more alike than he thinks.

I glance to my right and see a small camera in the corner of the room, and I know it's recording. I wonder if he'll sit in that chair of his and rewatch this in his free time—the two of us holding and comforting each other, content in the moment together.

I hope he watches it and feels the same as I do now.

# CHAPTER EIGHT

## LEX

I wake up pressed against a sleeping William. He's lying on his stomach facing me, the pillow cradled in his arms.

God, he's a sight. All those freckles, the red hair and fair skin.

I run my hand along his broad shoulders and feel my cock jump to attention. I am so fucking attracted to him, just a total goner.

I have felt this way in exactly *never*.

My mind flashes to him sitting between my legs last night, our hands interlocked—I've never done that before either, and fuck if I didn't enjoy it—and then I remember how he opened up and gave me just a small glimpse into his past.

Why did he share that with me? Was he hoping I'd open up and bare it all, like some kind of reciprocal bullshit?

I never fucking do that. Not for anyone. Except with Emery, but he's my best friend and we basically grew up together. So those revelations happened organically, especially with all those terrible nightmares he had. But at the moment, I don't have any inclination to share my shitty life story with anyone.

But I'd just assumed William had it all together. That his life was picture-perfect. Even though Brenda had hinted multiple times that it wasn't.... Fuck me.

I'm dense. I should have known what she was trying to tell me. I guess I didn't want to hear it. It was easier to hate him when I thought his life was grand.

My fingers slide down his spine and William arches into it, his eyes still closed in sleep.

I shift a little closer and breathe him in.

Mmm.

Bubblegum.

My finger slides to his sizable, bitable ass and I slip it through his crack.

His eyes pop open and they meet mine, his blue depths hazy from sleep.

"Good morning, sunshine," I say with a sly smile, my finger pressing against his hole.

His cheeks flush pink. I love watching them change colors.

"Lexington," he rasps and there it is. My cock, full mast. It wants inside of him. Badly.

"The way you say my name is so hot. Will you moan it when I fuck you?" I ask softly, my hands trembling at the thought of it.

William's cheeks darken and my smile widens.

I play with him a little more, until he turns his face into the pillow, groaning. I love how eager he is, how into me he seems to be. I haven't had anyone this far gone for me in...

well, ever. Most fucks I have with strangers are quick and mechanical, a means to get off.

And with Emery, it was just something we did because we were friends.

It was friendly and easy.

But none of this describes William. No, whatever this is, is so much more. So much better.

On top of it all, he seems to want to get to know me, and I am definitely just as curious about him.

Another low groan escapes him and I bite down on my bottom lip, wanting to play with him all day. I could spend hours and hours just focused on his ass, but we have actual shit to do today.

Slowly, I pull my hand away and he turns his head and blinks at me, his pupils blown out, the blue of his eyes just a thin ring.

God, he begs me for what he wants in silence, and I can read his need plain as fucking day.

"Oh, love. I'll take care of you later," I say, rolling off the bed and reluctantly standing up. William's eyes track my movements and I realize that I enjoy having them on me. I want them on me all the time.

"Shower time, William. And then we're getting your grandma and we're taking her for a fucking walk."

His eyebrows lower and I put a hand on my hip.

"She needs the exercise."

I half-expect him to argue, but instead, he just pushes himself up and then he's standing before me, blushing and completely naked.

He wets his lips, his eyes sliding down to my dick, and I internally curse myself for being so responsible because now I'm remembering how good that blow job was last night.

He looks like he wants to do it again...well, who am I to stop him?

"Come here," I say, holding out my hand.

I pull him into the bathroom, turn on the shower, and tug him inside.

When we're under the warm spray, I push him to his knees and he sinks down eagerly.

Once again, he sucks me down so enthusiastically I almost stumble over. I grab onto the shower bar to steady myself as his fingernails sink into my ass cheeks, hauling me into him. Over and over.

My eyes roll back in my head, and I'm desperately trying to retain some semblance of composure, but I am a total goner.

It feels too good. I can't hold back.

———

"Brenda," I say with an arched eyebrow, eyeing the short, fiery-haired woman beside me. "I am not getting you another fucking custard donut. Absolutely not."

She eyeballs me and then turns to the woman behind the counter and orders that shit right in front of me.

The gall of this woman.

"We came here to get you in shape, dammit, not stuff your face. It's bad enough that Vikki ordered extra fucking frosting for the cinnamon roll and did you see the mountain of brown sugar Martha is currently consuming?"

These women give zero fucks about their health. My anxiety is through the roof about it. William was a nice distraction last night, but when we showed up at Brenda's door this morning, she just looked so weak and tired.

And now I'm fucking worried all over again.

At this rate, I'll perish before her.

William clears his throat and my attention is snapped to the ridiculously handsome man just behind Brenda, his hands stuffed in his pockets, his blue eyes on me.

He's pulled his lips between his teeth, his eyes sparkling as he watches this battle of the wills unfold, but it's not fucking funny. This is dire. Life-threatening. Their cholesterol levels are rising as we speak.

"William," I say sharply. "Tell her. She can't fucking have it."

He shakes his head. "She can have another donut, Lexington. It's okay."

God, when he says my name I slowly begin to melt. Brenda, of course, catches all of this because she is staring at us with a knowing smirk.

"Lexington, hmm?" she asks, her eyes wide with delight. Oh, she didn't miss how William called me by my full name or the way he keeps ogling me.

I reach out and flick his arm, but it doesn't stop him. He just reaches out and hands her the damn donut that they stuffed with extra custard and then leads her to the table.

I am going to get him back for this.

I will enjoy torturing him later...if I don't pass out from the stress of it all.

"Took you long enough," Martha says, upending a spoonful of brown sugar in her mouth. She straight-up ordered this shit. It was supposed to be oatmeal with a side of brown sugar. But no, she just said, "I want the oatmeal, sans oatmeal. Just bring me the straight brown sugar." I mean, sugar packets are one thing, but a cereal bowl full of this shit is where I draw the line.

I try to reach for her spoon, but she kicks me under the table, hard.

I narrow my eyes at her, my shin throbbing

"That was not nice," I say but she just smiles at me.

Wicked woman.

And do not even get me started on Vikki. She's already scraped her plate clean, knowing I'd portion off that ginormous cinnamon roll. It was as big as her fucking head. They could stick some flowers on that thing and call it a wedding cake.

I'm going to email the Better Business Bureau and put them on blast. This is a health hazard.

"Oh hell, I needed that," Vikki says, setting her fork down and leaning back, patting her round stomach.

"You all are a bad example. You know we came to an agreement about how much sugar we can have, and you all just broke the fucking rules," I say as William sips his coffee, watching me lose my ever-loving shit.

Yes, well enjoy the show, William. I have been managing this chaos for six months while you lived with the alligators in Florida.

I am doing the best I fucking can.

"We are living our last days to the fullest. Marie Kondo says we should do this," Vikki blurts loudly.

"Yes, does this spark joy?" Martha replies, spooning another heap of brown sugar into her mouth. "Hell yes it does."

I reach over the table and swipe that spoon right out of her hand.

"That is meant for clothes and appliances, not sugary shit," I mutter.

"Same thing, Lex," Brenda says, licking her fingers.

Motherfucking Christ. Did she eat the whole donut that quickly? She could have choked.

"William," I say through gritted teeth. "You should have been monitoring this. What is wrong with you?"

"I thought you encouraged the bad behavior," he quips.

Oh, so now he wants to open that sexy mouth and talk?

My eye twitches when the corner of his mouth turns up. He thinks this is funny. I will show him funny when we get home.

"How did I encourage *this*?" I ask through clenched teeth and a false smile.

"The last time we went out to eat you drank mini-creamers and ate sugar packets with them. I thought it was the norm."

"Yes, well we have *limits,* which they've obviously forgotten about. They're breaking *all the rules*."

Martha suddenly burps loudly and William glances around, sliding a little lower in his seat, his cheeks firetruck red.

Good, he can be humiliated. I hope Martha keeps burping. She has it in her. I've heard it. It's impressive, like a bullhorn. And William deserves it for letting Brenda swallow that donut like a snake eating a mouse.

"Bren," I say quietly, tilting my head down toward her and getting a whiff of her signature perfume. "Seriously, you can't eat shit like this. It's not good for you. And William said you have a doctor's appointment coming up. What if something bad happens before then?"

She squeezes my hand. "I'm fine. I feel fine. And I wanted the donuts, Lex. Life is short, let me live a little."

I eye her. I mean, she looks fine. Better actually than she

did this morning when William and I showed up. Maybe the donut helped.

Oh, fuck me. Now I'm conflicted. What if a donut a day keeps the doctor away?

"Fine, but we are all taking a nice long walk after this," I declare.

It's the only way to make me feel better.

Martha groans and Vikki sighs heavily because neither of them wants to move unless it's toward sugar. They're like ants.

Another bullhorn burp escapes Martha and William practically disappears into his seat as people start to stare.

Vikki cackles evilly and Brenda smiles up at me.

"He can't keep his eyes off of you. Even half under the table," she tells me.

"Yes, well, we all know it's because I'm fabulous."

His blue eyes peek out from the under the tabletop, and I sigh.

"William, what the hell are you doing?" I bite out.

He scoots up a little, his fair skin practically glowing in mortification. God, I love that look on him. It's so fucking sexy. But I am still mad at him.

I have to remember that. Bad William. Bad donut.

"Okay, listen, ladies. No more burping or eating unhealthy shit. We are going for that walk, now," I say, taking pity on William. His skin is just going to melt right off of him.

"After I finish my coffee," Brenda says and takes a big, dramatic sip.

I roll my eyes but ultimately let her do whatever the hell she wants. And the entire time we sit there, William runs his foot across my calf. I like that he's playing footsie with me while making casual conversation with my ladies.

I've never done this before and it's turning me on more than I thought it would.

When we finally start moving, I am prepared to fight William for my chance to walk with Brenda, but he moves to Vikki instead, offering her his arm, and I slump in relief.

Fuck, he did that on purpose.

Maybe I'm not so mad at him after all.

Maybe I actually like him.

"He likes you too," Brenda says, suddenly a mind reader.

"I know."

"He's a good man," she adds. "I will feel so much better knowing the two of you have each other…"

I cut her off, my eyes stinging. "Stop it, Bren. *Stop. It.*"

She just looks at me with empathy, like she fucking knows I'm being naive, and my heart drops. For a moment, I can't breathe.

She can't know, can she? She has years left. Years.

She just tightens her hold on me and leans in, her head on my shoulder as we make our way through the air-conditioned mall.

I look at her tuft of ruby hair and feel my stomach clench.

Ten years. Ten fucking years left.

I decree it.

———

After dropping the ladies off, I drive us back to my apartment. I'm quieter than normal after our walk through the mall and William can tell. He watches me cautiously, his hands fisted in his lap. And, of course, he's completely silent.

"Are you okay?" he asks softly as I park my car and turn it

off. The heat of the summer is almost stifling, and I can't sit another moment in this damn car.

I push my way out and William follows, his footsteps soft and steady behind mine.

"I'm just in a funk, is all," I mutter as I push my apartment door open and step through. The AC hits me and I breathe a sigh of relief.

"I've never seen you this quiet," he says.

"Yes, well you've known me a week, so this is a first, William. I have bad days."

He watches me carefully and then takes a step toward me and my breath stutters out of my chest. One of his hands reaches out and envelopes mine. So fucking strong, and yet so gentle.

"What happened?" he asks.

My eye twitches and I look away from him. Jesus. I will not fucking lose my shit around this man.

Absolutely not.

I only lose my shit in privacy.

"I am not telling you," I mutter, and he squeezes my hand a little tighter and I feel my hard outer shell fracturing just a little.

"You seemed upset after talking to Grandma. What did she say?"

I pull my hand away from his and stalk to the kitchen, grabbing a glass and the whiskey. I need something to distract me from this horrifying conversation.

When I turn around, William is standing right where I left him, his eyes on me.

"Brenda just keeps talking about...." I can't even get the words out.

William rolls his lips between his teeth, but he doesn't say anything. I've never had anyone listen to me so raptly before.

"She keeps talking about dying," the last word comes out in a whisper and I take a large, burning sip of whiskey.

William moves toward me and gently takes the cup from my hand, setting it on the counter.

"I don't want to talk about it anymore," I grumble as his hands slide up my chest and clasp onto the back of my neck. Mine go to his hips and I pull him into me.

"She's fine. And the doctor's appointment is in a few days and then you can hear it for yourself," he says soothingly.

My eyes shut and I tilt my head back a little, letting out a exhale.

I know all this; I just have this bad fucking feeling. It's probably just my anxiety rearing its ugly head. But I've never had anyone in my life like her before.

I can't imagine my life without her in it.

"Hey," he says softly, his nose nuzzling the line of my jaw. "It's okay, Lexington."

I can't stand it, how kind he's being right now. It makes my chest hurt.

"Here," William says, and my eyes pop open when I feel him nudge my arm.

I look down at his extended hand and see the flash drive in his palm.

"What's this?" I ask, my brows furrowed.

He meets my confused stare. "I don't want it."

I just gape at him in disbelief because seriously? Who is this man? I would be all over that info. I would be analyzing that shit to death.

"Why the fuck not?" I ask, feeling a little offended. Does

he not want to know me? I basically handed him a highly confidential account of my past.

Does he not care?

"I want *you* to tell me, Lexington. When you're ready."

Well, motherfucker. I was not expecting that and I hate that I like it.

I glower at him, feeling my heart thunder in my chest. My eyes sting.

"Yes, well, you won't get to know me unless you read this. I'm not going to tell you any of my shit."

He bites his inner cheek and examines me. Then I see him set the flash drive down on the counter.

"You will."

I scoff and roll my eyes because the nerve of this man. I will *never*.

He pulls my face toward his, brushing his lips against mine, and I pull him into me because he tastes good.

And he's being fucking *nice*. Absolutely disgustingly nice.

I need this to move in a different direction before I start blubbering.

Tilting my head, I push my tongue into his mouth and glide it against his, feeling his cock hardening against me.

"My bedroom, now," I mutter against his lips.

We stumble toward it, our mouths chasing each other's, not wanting to be parted for a second. Damn, he's getting better at kissing. Pretty soon he'll be a pro.

I tug him in closer.

He won't be kissing anyone else but me.

His mouth is mine. His whole body is mine.

I didn't have parents and I never learned how to share.

We fall onto the bed and rut against each other, tearing off clothes frantically. His eyes are hooded, his cheeks redder than ever. He looks like a fucking wet dream, one I never want to wake up from. I roll us until I'm on top and our bare cocks slide against each other.

Fuck, we look good like this.

"Lexington," William moans, leaning up to press his mouth against mine, his hand on my ass, pulling me into him over and over.

God, he's so eager. I've never had anyone this desperate for me. It makes me want to come all over him, mark him as mine.

I push up on my arms and stare down at him, all lush lips and freckles.

"I want to show you something," I say, my voice gravelly.

His Adam's apple bobs, and he nods, his fingers flexing against my ass.

I love what a good student he is. He's so willing to learn.

Leaning over, I grab the lube from the nightstand.

I roll to my side a little and drip some of the gel onto his cock and then move back onto him. Our dicks are pressed against each other, and William exhales shakily.

"Put your hand around us and jerk us together."

His chest heaves as he does what I say, and the minute our cocks are tight together as his fist is working us both toward the edge, I just let my eyes close and escape into the feeling of it.

"Perfect. Fucking perfect," I huff as his hand slides up and down our lengths. "You're such a good boy. So good for me."

I open my eyes and find his gaze locked on my face. He looks so damn beautiful, and I can't help but smile down at him. He smiles back and oh, my heart.

I lean down and catch his mouth in a bruising kiss.

"Like butterscotch," I mutter, licking into him again and again, and sucking on his tongue.

He's whimpering now, his wrist working faster and faster, his breathing labored.

I'm not much better off; I'm thrusting wildly and groaning into his mouth as I near the edge.

I feel William's body tense and warm wetness gushes between us. His release spurs me on and I spill onto his stomach.

When we're done, we both just lie there catching our breath, neither of us able or willing to move.

"Was that good?" he asks so innocently. Oh, he has no idea what he does to me.

I lift my head to meet his gaze and press a kiss to the tip of his nose. Never done that before, but it feels right.

"Fucking fabulous."

He smiles up at me, looking satisfied and...happy.

He slowly lets our dicks go and brings his hand up to his mouth, licking his cum-covered fingers. And when he presses his thumb against my mouth, I clean it thoroughly with my tongue.

Oh, I love this filthy part of him.

"Will you watch this when you're alone?" he asks shyly.

"Of course I will."

He looks away from me and bites down on his bottom lip.

"Good."

Sweet Jesus, this man.

I roll off of him to get some space because I am about to fucking lose it, but he just follows me over, his body pressed against my side.

He watches me quietly, and I can't fucking help myself, I just wrap an arm around him and pull him against me.

His head lands softly on my shoulder and his leg is thrown over mine.

As he plays with my belly button ring, he asks, "Is it true you don't have people over like this? That I'm your first?"

I swallow. "Yes, that's true. I am very picky about who I let into my life."

His finger stills and then resumes playing with my ring.

"I am too."

When I don't say anything, he adds, "We are more similar than you think."

"Apparently. Brenda likes to hint at it, though she's never really told me how."

He stills once more.

"I grew up in a trailer park," he says, and oh shit, I don't even breathe because I want to hear every word he utters. He rarely speaks, so when he does, I hang on every word. "Growing up I saw a lot of drugs, sex...things little kids shouldn't see."

"Same," I grumble.

"My teacher called CPS when she saw the bruises. That's when I went to live with my grandma."

I sigh. "Yes, well I'm glad you had her. That you at least had someone to go to. I spent most of my teenage years in foster care."

William shifts and leans up, looking down at me.

"Where are your parents?"

"You could just look at the damn flash drive I gave you."

He leans down and presses a soft kiss to my lips and pulls the answer right out of me.

"My mom died from an overdose. My dad is incarcerated for murder."

He blinks down at me but doesn't say a word. He rests his

head back on my shoulder and runs his fingers across the tattoos on my abdomen.

"Mine are still alive, but I haven't had contact with them in years."

"Yes, well, why would you when you have Brenda?"

He's silent again and I've come to realize how much he thinks before speaking. It makes what he says seem so much more appealing.

He's the complete opposite of my best friend, Emery, who rattles off every damn thing that crosses his mind.

"Do you have any other family?" he asks.

"No. All I have is Emery and Brenda. And that's all I need."

William sighs against me, his breath tickling my skin.

"And me," he whispers.

Why, yes, it seems that I do.

# CHAPTER NINE



## LEX

The next morning, I awaken to William's warm, naked body curled around mine. I've never really been spooned before—it feels safe and comforting, like my own personal cocoon—and in this moment, I decide that I like waking up with someone like this. Waking up with *him*.

I trace a finger across his bicep and watch it flex slightly under my touch.

Last night, things between us felt like they shifted.

It seems that sharing about our similar pasts made me like William more than I already did.

Shit. What comes next? A committed relationship?

I've never had one of those.

This whole thing started out as me attempting to give William all his firsts. But, damn, it seems like he's given me just as many. What's one more? What would it really hurt?

I turn my head and stare at the ceiling.

Well, I guess I'm keeping him because the thought of him with someone else makes me want to rage.

And if for some reason, he tires of me and casts me aside, I'll just have to stalk him. I really am no better than Susana.

I kind of, sort of, mostly understand why that bitch acts the way she does. William is just so easy to obsess over. There is just something about him.

All that quiet innocence makes you want to wreck him.

I carefully roll out of his hold and off of the bed and move into the bathroom to take a piss and brush my teeth. I plan on making out with him for a while this morning before I leave to take care of some things.

As I am putting toothpaste on my toothbrush, William walks in, eyeing my ass. I arch an eyebrow at him, and he blushes.

That will never get old. Not in a million years.

"Good morning, sunshine, I mumble around my toothbrush.

"Morning," he says softly.

I straight up stare as he pees. Yes, I am a creep, but I cannot pull my eyes away. I also watch as he washes his hands. It seems my eyes cannot stop tracking him now that I've decided he's mine.

I rinse my toothbrush and then hand it to him.

When he hesitates, I roll my eyes. "You licked my cum off your fingers last night, and I have excellent dental hygiene."

He huffs out a laugh and then proceeds to brush his teeth. I watch it all in exaggerated detail.

When he's finished rinsing out his mouth, he moves toward me, wrapping me in his strong arms and pressing gentle kisses to my collarbones.

My heart just melts in my chest. Stupid ice cream heart.

"I have to take care of some things this morning," I say, threading my fingers through his hair and tugging on it softly to pull his face up to mine. "And then after work, come over. I am going to do things to you, William. We have some more things we need to practice to get them absolutely perfect."

He glances up at me and I smirk back at him. He has no idea what's in store for him.

I have plans. Big ones. I'm going to work him up to it nice and slow.

"I'm going to the gym for a bit after work and then...can we grab dinner first?" he asks, and I wet my lips because if it were up to me, I'd eat him for the main course.

"Of course, love."

And when our lips meet, he tastes like a York Peppermint Patty.

————

It was harder to leave William than I expected. I've never had that problem before. Usually, I can't get away fast enough. But of course, everything with William is different.

We kissed for an exorbitant amount of time in the parking garage before wrenching our lips away from each other. Neither of us wanted to leave.

I'm not even mad about it.

Now I'm currently outside of Susana's apartment, waiting for Diablo to arrive. I glance at my phone and roll my eyes.

Always fucking late.

So inconsiderate of my time.

Plus, the heat. It's so fucking hot and it's only nine o'clock.

He does this on purpose, I guarantee it. He probably looked at the weather report and cackled.

A minute later, I hear the scraping of his car as it comes around the corner. This kid refuses to give up this hunk of decaying metal. It's as old as dirt and barely runs, but he is a fucking stubborn asshole.

It jerks and comes to a sputtering stop in front of me and I stare in exasperation at the sky.

Why, oh why am I friends with this heathen?

"Your family is as rich as fuck and here you are, driving the car equivalent of a rotting zombie," I mutter when Diablo pops out of the front seat. He's small, and despite being close to my age, looks like a prepubescent teen. He's wearing a baggy shirt and oversized pants that are so long they pool around his sneakers. His hair is a bit of a mess and, I lean forward, is that food on his cheek?

He could do with a makeover. And a shower.

Still, even though he's a hot mess, I'd never mess with him.

Speaking of people you shouldn't mess with, a behemoth exits the passenger side of the car and the vehicle actually squeaks and shakes as this man steps out.

As he stands silently facing us with his arms crossed, I notice his clean-cut, dirty-blond hair, short beard, and green eyes, but my eyes are immediately drawn to his massive biceps. They're thicker than my waist.

Jesus, this man must be some kind of genetic impossibility. Was he created in a lab? Is he some kind of government weapon?

"Who the fuck is this?" I ask, waving my hand at the towering giant next to me, because I sure as fuck haven't seen him before. I would have noticed.

"This is Skylar. My dad insisted he come along," Diablo

says with an exasperated huff. "Apparently there are issues in the *family*. So, I'm saddled with this orc for a few days."

I eyeball the large man who seems unbothered by Diablo's description of him. I mean, Diablo isn't wrong. "Well, he is impressive. Although, Skylar isn't a very fitting name."

"I know. Who the fuck thought that was a good idea?" Diablo replies with a snort. "I mean, look at him."

"You could name swap," I blurt, and Diablo snaps his gaze to mine.

"Be fucking nice, Lex. Or I won't let Skylar break any bones."

"Who said I wanted any bones broken?"

He puts a hand on his hip and narrows his eyes at me. "You are too soft, Lex. My father would be very disappointed in you. Now, I hope you have what I want because we had an agreement."

"Of course. I never fucking break my word."

I pop the trunk of my car and pull out a clear container, handing it to him.

He opens the top and peers inside. "Nice work, Lex. I am *never* disappointed."

He reaches in and pulls out a small *Warhammer* figurine that I hand painted the other night.

"Everyone is so envious," Diablo says with glee. "No one knows my secret weapon."

I puff up a little because yes, I paint mini figurines in my free time, and yes, I am fucking superb at it. I really should have my own YouTube channel. Not that I have the time for that.

Diablo snaps the container shut and locks it in his trunk before moving to stand near me. Skylar, meanwhile, hasn't moved or said anything. He just hovers, watching Diablo with an intensity that makes me a little nervous. He's taking his job *very* seriously.

"Can he move quickly?" I whisper.

"I have no idea," Diablo grumbles. "Though I doubt it. He's too big to move fast. I can just see him lumbering about."

"Well, worse comes to worst, you could hide behind him if something goes awry," I say, taking note of his thick legs and large torso.

"I think that's the plan. Anyways, this is boring. Can we please get on with the fun stuff?"

He eyeballs the entrance of the apartment and then Skylar.

"Skylar, grab the stuff," he commands, and Skylar moves to the backseat of the car with a lot more grace than I expected, and grabs a duffle bag.

"Do you have what *I* need?" I ask as Skylar throws the bag over his beefy shoulder.

Diablo hands me a file folder, slapping it down in my open palm.

"Always, now let's scare this bitch," he says with an evil rub of his hands.

He takes too much pleasure in other people's pain. One day this kid is going to meet his match.

We walk up the stairs because the elevator is out of order, and then we're standing right in front of our destination.

So, this is where Susana lives, huh? I wasn't sure what I was expecting, but nothing quite so dreary and drab.

I knock on the door and am pleasantly surprised when it opens rather quickly. I hate waiting. It puts me in a mood.

"I'm not interested," a middle-aged woman says, eyeing us with annoyance. She has boring brown hair and nondescript eyes. Her outfit is atrocious. No wonder William wasn't interested.

I am much more fun.

Am I being petty? Probably. Do I care? Not one iota.

"Susana?" I ask sweetly, baring my teeth at her.

Her eyes meet mine and she nods but before she can say another word, Diablo is pushing into her apartment.

"Let's kill this bitch," he says with an evil cackle.

Her mouth falls open in shock as Skylar follows him in, jostling her slightly.

I sigh loudly, shaking my head, as I enter the apartment, because could we not do this a little more covertly? I don't know why I thought we could. Quickly, I close the door behind me and lock it.

"Excuse them. They're so rude."

Skylar drops the bag to the ground and Diablo crouches down.

"Get the fucking rope, Skylar. Tie this cunt up."

Her eyes are wide and I think at this moment, she's starting to panic. Because the duffle bag is zipped open and, Jesus fucking Christ...

"Diablo, did you seriously bring the saws? I told you we're not doing this shit," I grumble. This guy is ridiculous. I mean, how many does he even have in there? Ten? Who needs that many saws?

I could do a lot of things with just one good, sturdy one.

Diablo rolls his eyes at me as a high-pitched scream begins to bubble out of the woman's throat. Ah yes, now it is sinking in.

Skylar moves quicker than I expect. He reaches over and slaps a massive hand over her mouth, stifling her voice. He then lifts her up, tying her to a chair and stuffing a rag in her mouth.

Oh my god, I am going to jail for this.

Crazy bastards.

"We could do this without the theatrics," I mutter as I watch Skylar move to the kitchen to wash his hands.

"Yes, well this is more fun," Diablo says, pulling an electric saw out of his bag and searching for an outlet to plug it in.

"They make those cordless now, you know," I say. "Really, that is so inefficient. What if you had to dismember someone outdoors?"

Diablo sighs. "I know, but this is what they had in stock, Lex. *Skylar*," he calls out. "Find a plug for me. Chop, chop."

Skylar obeys without even so much as a grumble, and I wonder where Diablo's dad found this guy. He's good. Very, very good.

"Ignore them," I tell a now-crying Susana. There is a literal snot bubble coming out of her nose and I cringe, backing away. Don't want that popping and getting on me. I don't do hazardous waste.

"Keep it together. No one is chopping you up," I tell her.

"You don't know that," Diablo says, moving around the small space, waving the saw around dramatically.

"Well, not yet, at least." I crouch down before her. "Now," I say, holding out the file in front of me. "Do you know William?"

Her eyes widen and I smile at her.

"Ah, yes, I know you do because I've seen the messages you've been sending him. Very inappropriate, if I may say so."

She shakes her head frantically and I sigh. "Look, I'm going to lay it out for you. William is mine, not yours. Your interfering is really making him uncomfortable, so here I am... solving this...*problem.*"

She nods, aiming to please, but I'm not done. I need to explain this so she can understand how serious I am.

Suddenly, the saw motor starts up in the background and I roll my eyes. My god, Diablo is a crazy person. Crazier than me.

I blame his family. They did this. This is all nurture right here.

"Susana, here is the deal. You are going to leave William alone. And by alone, I mean that you're not going to call him, text him, or show up within two miles of him, ever again."

She tries talking but her words are muffled by the rag. And truth is, I'm not here to chat. I'm here to lay out my terms and then sic Diablo on her when she breaks them.

"Do you understand?"

She nods and I sigh. Thank god. I am over this already. I just want to get on with my day.

"Now, as a little incentive, because really, what incentive do you have to listen to me? None at all. So as of this moment, you, Susana, are officially dead."

She shakes her head again crying, and *I swear to god*, is that saw getting louder? I turn around and see an electric saw in each of Diablo's hands.

"Turn that shit off, Diablo! Motherfuck! I can't fucking think," I shout.

"Do not speak to me like that. Or I'll have Skylar smash you," he grunts, but thankfully the saws cut off and I turn to face a trembling Susana. Well, I'd feel bad if she didn't deserve it.

This bitch had it coming.

"Like I said. *Dead.*" I show her the death certificate in

my hand. "Now, you're already technically six feet under, so if I find out you were in contact with my William again, no one will miss you when we come back to kill you for real. Because you are currently kaput and you're going to stay that way."

She starts trying to talk again and I smack her in the leg with her death certificate as hard as I can.

"Shut up and listen."

She stills, a tear leaking out of her eye.

"If you don't leave him alone, with just a push of a button, you will disappear. Your bank records, your credit cards, your birth certificate, your social security number, everything. It'll be like you never existed. And then you'll be disposed of for good. Do you understand me?"

She nods and I stand up, placing my hands on my hips, and look around.

"This place needs a major renovation. I suggest you move. Find something nicer. Far, far away." I glance down at her. "Do you understand?"

She nods dramatically and I add, "And do not even bother reporting this. You'll get nowhere."

"No-where," Diablo parrots. "Now can we go? This is boring. Especially if I can't use the saws."

I glance at Diablo and shake my head. "Yeah, let's go."

"I have things to do. People to see." I set the death certificate on the table and glance back at Susana.

"Far, far away. No contact," I repeat because I really don't want to have her killed.

Hopefully she takes us seriously.

But I wouldn't feel that bad making her disappear if push comes to shove.

Diablo packs up his saws, and a few minutes later we're

making our way back outside, squinting in the bright morning sun.

"Well, that was a lot of drama for a Tuesday. Were the saws really necessary?" I ask him.

"I know," he says. "But it made her take us seriously. And with my height and general appearance, I need the fucking saws, Lex."

I give an understanding nod. "Touché."

"Now, Skylar and I have a game meet at ten. So, we need to fucking scoot."

Skylar wordlessly moves toward the car with Diablo and I watch in disbelief as he scrunches inside.

That poor man. Hopefully he's getting paid enough for this.

I glance down at my phone, swipe at the screen, and pull up the video feed of William's office.

Ah. Tsk, tsk.

Such a bad boy.

I see what you're doing, William. I see what those hands are doing.

I've decided my next client can wait. I'm going to make a pit stop.

# CHAPTER TEN



## WILLIAM

It's been two days and Susana hasn't contacted me at all and I keep staring at Lex wondering what the fuck he did.

I can't bring myself to ask, though, because I'm not sure I want to know.

"What are you thinking in that sexy head of yours?" he asks, quirking an eyebrow at me.

We're naked in bed, my body covered in a sheen of sweat, still flushed red from the exertion of writhing underneath him.

It hasn't grown old in the least. He could gently whisper his hands along me and I'd come.

I pull my swollen, well-kissed lips between my teeth and meet his stare.

"Nothing."

He rolls his eyes and presses a kiss to my shoulder, nipping me lightly.

"Tell me, William. Don't keep secrets from me."

His hand is splayed across my stomach, smearing our mess into my skin. God, the things he did to me with his tongue.

"I was just thinking about Susana."

His hand stills and he narrows his eyes.

"Is that so? What about her?"

I wet my lips and his gaze tracks the movement. He seems to want me just as much as I want him. When he's on me, he's ravenous, hungry for more. He can't pull his body away from mine. I can sense the desperation in him.

"What did you do to her?" I ask softly, my hand moving up his bicep and cupping his neck.

"Do you really want to know?" he asks, throwing a leg over mine and propping his head in his hand. He glances down at me, his fingers drawing circles on my skin.

"I'm not sure."

"Well, then let me just put it this way...she's not dead. Not physically anyways. But she should be leaving you alone. In fact, she should be far, far away from here by now. Why? Has she contacted you?"

I shake my head, my fingers tugging on the strands of his silver hair.

"No."

"Good, you let me know if she does, William. Because I'll make her go away. No one hurts you. Ever."

Ugh, why is that so sexy? I lean up and press my lips to his.

When we pull away minutes later, Lex flops onto his back.

"William, just so you know, you taste fantastic. You always do. Is this some kind of special mouthwash you use?"

I let out a soft chuckle. "No."

"Then you must be some kind of genetic anomaly. Because you always taste like sweetness."

I press a kiss to his chest and then finally wrench my hands away. I sit up and reach over for some tissues, wiping myself up.

"Want to order dinner?" I ask.

He turns his head to look at me. "Actually, I was thinking we could head to my best friend's house for dinner. He invited us yesterday. Would you like to do that?"

Suddenly, I feel nervous. I'm not really good with people. Numbers are more my forte. They don't ask me personal questions or expect me to be charming.

"Is this the one that saw us naked?" I ask

"Yes, but it's not like he hasn't seen me nude before."

I stare at him, and he must see the question in my eyes because he explains. "If you must *pry* it out of me. We had sexual relations, William. But that ended ages ago, so don't worry your pretty little head."

*What the hell*, I think as my stomach clenches. I don't like that at all.

Lex smirks a little. "Are you jealous?"

Of course I am, and I don't even know why. I know Lex has had sex before me. I just can't help but *hate* it.

"You are. But let me tell you..." Lex says, moving toward me and threading his fingers through my hair. "I have never been addicted to anyone like I am to you."

My breath hitches and I meet his steady gaze.

"You have nothing to worry about."

I nod and let him lead me into the bathroom where we take turns washing each other, and then dress to leave.

"Now a word about my best friend..." Lex begins as we make our way across town in his car.

"You mean, the one you fucked," I interject, and Lex sighs.

"My god, when you do speak, you are so snarky. Yes, that

one. We grew up together, okay? We fucked as a means to an end. It was nothing more. Now...back to what I was going to say. He's different, so just roll with it. August usually reins him in, but there is a chance he'll let him go off the rails, in which case, we just need to nod our heads and let him chug along into the distance."

I bob my head, not quite sure what to make of all that.

"And his boyfriend, August, is very hot, as you well know. I'd appreciate it if you didn't gape and ogle him in front of me. At least do it when I'm not looking."

My eyebrows meet because what the fuck is he talking about? I'm not attracted to anyone but him. Doesn't he know this? I haven't told him, have I? I just assumed he knew.

"Lexington."

He groans next to me, adjusting his pants in the process.

"Jesus, when you say my name like that."

I huff out a laugh because he's utterly ridiculous. "Lexington, I don't see anyone else when you're around."

"Oh, fuck off."

"I'm serious. Why do you think I've never...done anything with anyone before?"

His foot eases off the gas pedal and he quickly eyes me.

"I wasn't interested in anything like that until I saw *you*."

He blows out a long breath, his fingers tapping a nervous rhythm on the steering wheel.

"Well, feel free to shower me with compliments any day of the week. I love hearing what you think of me."

"Okay. I can do that," I say softly, and Lex reaches out and threads his fingers with mine.

"Would you like to know what I think of you?"

I nod, feeling my entire arm tingle from his touch.

"Well, I think you're hot as fuck. All that red hair and those freckles…"

I shift in my seat, my dick hardening just from the sound of his voice.

"And your physique. I just want to touch you everywhere. How is an accountant this hot? I don't know, William. I just don't fucking know. When we get home, I would very much like to fuck you."

*Oh god, yes.*

I press my palm against my hard dick, willing it to go down. I don't want to meet his best friend for the second time with this damn thing poking out from my pants. It was bad enough that I was naked the first time.

"Would you let me fuck you?" he asks and my head flops back against the headrest. Because yes, *yes* I would. I'd let him do whatever he wanted to me. Doesn't he know that already?

"You can do whatever you want to me," I nearly moan and then bring our entwined hands up to my mouth and lick at his fingers. Like an animal.

I am just so fucking horny all the time.

When I bring my grandma to the doctor, I am going to have a quick, private chat with him to see what's wrong with me.

Because there is definitely something wrong with my dick.

Lex groans, suddenly jerking the steering wheel and pulling us off onto the side of the road. Gravel crunches beneath the tires as he slams the car into park. Then he's nearly crawling over the console, his lips finding mine, fucking his tongue into my mouth.

When we finally pull apart, what feels like hours later, we're both a mess. Rumpled clothes, mussed hair, swollen lips.

Swollen cocks.

"William," he says, panting slightly. "What the hell are we supposed to do with these?"

He waves to his crotch and then mine.

"You started it...by existing," I mutter, and Lex barks out a laugh.

"I would cancel dinner, but I can guarantee Emery would not let me live it down. I'd hear about it for weeks." He pauses. "No. I'd hear about it for years. It would be the ultimate betrayal."

He flops back down into his seat and sighs heavily.

"We have about five minutes to get our dicks under control, William. Do you think we can do that?"

I glance down at it, feeling a little helpless because I don't know if I can do it. It seems impossible. It's always hard now.

But by the time we're pulling up to the small one-story house in a quiet suburb, I'm so nervous my dick can't be bothered to perk up.

It's hiding in my pants.

Chicken.

I step out of the car and follow Lex up to the front door, trying my best to act normal, but failing. I don't people well. I spend too much time with numbers.

Numbers make sense. People do not.

Lex rings the doorbell and I hear a crash and then the door is flung open.

"Lex!" Emery says, a smile on his handsome face. "I thought you would bail."

"I would never, Eminem. I am a good, loyal friend."

Emery bounces from foot to foot and then swivels his head to meet my gaze.

"Hi there, stranger!"

I lift a hand in an awkward wave.

"Hi," I say, my voice rough and awkward. So I try again. "Hi."

There. More normal. Good. I can do this.

"Hello again. Come in. Let me take your coat. Very fancy," Emery says, reaching behind me to help me take it off, but his hands are slapped away by Lex's.

"Do not touch him, Eminem. Only I touch him."

Emery rolls his eyes as August rounds the corner.

"Hey," the handsome and very calm man says, his lips tilted up in a friendly smile.

"Hi, August," Lex says. "You remember William."

"Vaguely. I had my eyes closed the whole time."

"Yes, well, now you can meet him with your eyes open and really get a good look. This is handsome, sexy William. William this is August, Emery's boyfriend."

"Yes, mine. All mine," Emery says with a manic smile. "Now, look, I made dinner but let me tell you, I made a mistake..."

My eyebrows rise as he says, "Instead of a tablespoon of salt, I put in a half a cup. I know...I *know*. I don't know what I was thinking, but it happened, okay? So, we tossed it and ordered pizza. It should be here in like ten minutes. You want a drink?"

He rushes over to the kitchen and bumps into the wall as he goes. August just watches him go, hearts in his eyes and I feel suddenly so lost.

Is this how it is? Is this what love looks like? My grandma was the most normal adult in my life, but her husband had died, and she never remarried. I never got to see her with someone else. It was always just the two of us.

And for the first time in my life, I'm seeing what a relationship could be like. It's just a glimpse, but still. I can feel the adoration between them.

It doesn't always have to be like my parents, with the fighting and the anger and the abuse.

Perhaps that's why I never ended up with anyone, why I was never turned on by or wanted to be touched by another person, because I was protecting myself.

Except with Lex, my body finally took notice and woke the fuck up.

It said hello and it ain't saying goodbye...ever.

"Here," Emery thrusts a can of soda into my hand and then one into Lex's. I glance at the orange can, not recognizing the brand.

"Oh my god, Eminem. You remembered," Lex says with a gasp. "I haven't had this in ages."

"I know, right? We were talking about it the other week, and I swear to god, an angel reminded me about this when I was at the grocery store."

"I reminded him," August interjects, and Emery waves his hand in front of his face.

"Whatever. Same thing. No need to rub it in, August."

But August ignores him. "I actually had to go back to the store to buy it after he returned home without it."

Emery narrows his eyes at his boyfriend, who just smiles and pulls him into his side.

"What has gotten into you? You're being...sexily mean," Emery says, nuzzling into August's side. "I'm not sure if I like it."

"I'm not being mean, Em. I'm just teasing."

"Yes, well, I'm feeling conflicted about it. Mostly. Not really, but I could be feeling some way about it."

"I'm sorry," August says, pressing a soft kiss to the top of

Emery's head. I watch it all in awe, the orange soda hanging limply in my hand.

I look over at Lex and wonder...could what we have ever evolve into this? Right here, the nuzzling and sweet-talking?

God, I hope so.

Lex pops the can open and guzzles some down, smacking his lips.

"Satan, this is good. Brings back so many memories," he says, bringing everyone's focus on him.

"Right?" Emery drawls and then asks me, "Did Lex tell you that we grew up together? Well, mostly grew up together. In foster care..."

"Yeah," I say and then think, *and I know that you two fucked*, but I realize this isn't the time. Wait, scratch that. There isn't ever a time for that.

"Yeah, we've been friends for a long time," Emery says. "I could tell you secrets about him, William, if you want to know."

My entire body freezes and so does Lex's because he's narrowing his eyes at his best friend.

"I'd like that," I say, and Lex steps into my space, putting a hand around my arm and tugging me to the side.

"You will do no such thing, love," he says, the can of orange soda wielded between us like a weapon.

"It seems things just slip out of Emery," I say softly. "I wouldn't mind hearing a few...secrets of yours."

Lex leans closer to me. "You had the flash drive."

"I did."

"And you gave it back because you wanted *me* to tell you all the things."

"I do."

"But you're willing to let Emery divulge all."

"Not all," I reply. But I sure as fuck would take some if they happened to pop out of that wild mouth of his.

Lex's eyes move to my mouth and then back up to my eyes.

"Oh, you are mischievous. You constantly do the opposite of what I expect."

"I'm not and I don't."

And that's the truth. I'm unexciting and boring and just overall mundane.

"No. You're like a fox, so very clever."

I am clever. Sometimes. But not really that often.

I reach out and tug the can of soda from his hand and press it to my lips, taking a small, measured sip. I've never had orange soda before and I want my mouth to be anywhere near the vicinity of his. It's been too long since we've kissed.

Lex's eyes grow hooded as my throat works.

"Oh, you filthy..." Lex says, pulling his lip ring between his teeth.

"Guys?" Emery suddenly says. "Um, the pizza is here, and I know you are doing like a...mating ritual or something, but can we eat? I'm hungry and August said it would be rude to start without you."

Lex tugs the can of soda from my hand.

"Mating ritual...we'll see about that when we get home. I'll mate you all fucking night long."

Yes, do that, please.

Let's fuck like animals.

———

"Thank god we're almost home," Lex says, his hands tapping an uneven rhythm on the steering wheel.

We made it through dinner intact, Lex behaving himself, mostly, and me just listening intently. Just in off chance Emery had something he wanted to divulge.

And he did. Kind of.

Lex and he grew up in foster care—which I knew. What I didn't know is that they were roommates for years until Emery moved in with August. Growing up, Lex got into tech and surveillance after a creepy foster dad was lurking around outside his room at night.

I wanted him to go into more detail about this because it was a glimpse inside that head of his, but he'd cut Emery off abruptly. I mean, I don't need to know the gory details, I really don't, but I do want to know about his past and what his life has been like. It helps to give me insight into who he is today.

"Oh, go ahead," Lex mutters. "Go ahead and ask. I can see you're dying to do it."

I roll my lips between my teeth and say, "Is that really why you got into the tech field?"

"Yes, mostly. I wanted evidence of the shit those creepy fucks were doing. Saved up my money, bought some cameras and it evolved from there. I've always been good with computers. It just...it just fits me, and I do it well."

I nod because it *is* fitting.

"I don't want to go into more detail about it. They're not needed, but bad things happened and I fixed it. That's all you need to know."

"Okay," I say, running my hands along my thighs. "I get it."

He's silent for a moment and then asks, "And how did you get into accounting?"

I turn my gaze toward Lex as he pulls into his apartment complex. "Numbers always made sense to me."

"Yes, I can see that. People are complicated. You, on the other hand, are complicated in the best way."

He's mistaken. I'm not complicated at all. I'm just a simple guy who happens to be obsessed with Lex.

He shuts off the car and then looks at me, one of his hands reaching out to trace the outline of my lips.

"Let's go upstairs. I want to kiss you again."

"God yes," I say, nearly stumbling out of the car. He pulls me through the garage and up the stairs. When we burst through the door, he's on me. We don't even make it to the bed. We tumble onto the couch, our bodies threaded around each other, writhing. Fuck, he feels good on top of me. I want him inside of me.

He rips my shirt right off my head and then kisses his way down my chest and I arch up into him, my hands in his hair, pulling gently.

His groan echoes around the room as he rips his lips from mine and sits up, working our pants open.

"I want to fuck you," he breathes, and I just nod my acceptance. I'd let him do anything to me.

He stands up and shucks our pants off until we're both naked and I feel like my skin is on fire just from the sight of him, from knowing what's about to happen.

"But we need to work you open first. Stretch out that hole for me." I swallow roughly as he holds out his hand. "Come here, love."

Obediently, I link my fingers with his and he pulls me to the bedroom where he pushes me down onto the mattress.

He moves to the drawer by his nightstand and pulls out a small butt plug, and I know exactly what it is only because I looked it up this week, wondering how I'd fit his dick in my ass.

"I'm going to have you wear this for a bit," he explains as he kneels between my legs and spreads them open. It feels like forever ago when I was completely mortified by him staring at my ass.

*Look all you want, Lex. This hole is yours.*

He grabs the lube and dribbles some on the plug.

"And when you're comfortable with this, I'll replace it with my dick. But in the meantime, let's have some fun."

I feel the tip of the plug at my hole as he slowly pushes it inside. A gasp escapes me as he gently works it further and further inside of me. It's such a strange feeling, something going in that hole, but I don't hate it.

No, I fucking *like* it.

"Good boy," he mutters, pulling one of my legs up onto his shoulder. His mouth gently presses against my calf and I groan just having his lips on my skin. I want his mouth on me all the time.

Lex licks a line across my leg as he pushes the plug all the way into place until the base is snug against my opening.

"Mmm, there," he says, his eyes sliding down to where the plug is. "Perfect. Look at you."

He strokes my half-hard cock until it's fully erect again and leaking onto my abdomen.

"Can I take a picture of this so I can look at it later?" he asks, stroking the answer right out of me.

"Yeah," I breathe.

Lex smirks at me and then hops off the bed, grabbing his phone from his pants pocket.

And when he gets back, he spreads my legs, positioning the camera right at my ass and snapping a few pictures.

"Fuck me, William," he mutters. "You're a motherfucking

work of art." His eyes snap up to meet mine as he sets the phone down. "Will you wear this every day?"

"Yes."

"It's for your own good. I don't want to hurt you. But I want inside of you. Desperately."

"I know," I say, and Lex falls onto me, kissing me with palpable need, and the sensation of something inside of me only makes it more intense.

I love it. I'm going to love having him inside of me.

Our cocks converge as we rut against each other and then suddenly, Lex is sitting up, grabbing onto the lube and squirting it onto my dick. The feel of it, of his slick hand tightening around my dick, nearly makes me come.

But he squeezes the base of my cock before I can explode.

"Oh, not yet, William. First, I'm going to sit on you. I can't fucking wait another minute."

My breath completely leaves my body because *holy fuck*.

He's suddenly straddling me and my dick slides right up inside of him without any resistance. I don't even get a chance to inhale before I'm balls-deep in his tight ass.

"Lexington," I groan because I'm not going to last. He just needs to move once and I'm a goner. "I can't…" I gasp, my hands clutching onto his hips painfully hard, trying to hold him in place. "Don't move…I can't…," I cry out as he slides up my length and then slams back down.

My eyes nearly cross from the sensation, my entire body on fire. How am I ever going to go back to using my hand when I know what Lex's ass feels like? I'm completely ruined.

"You feel so good inside me. Fuck, yes. Your cock is mine. You're mine, all mine," he groans as he starts to move and that's it.

I don't last. I don't even try. It's futile anyway. This is Lex, after all.

I explode right into him, letting Lex work every drop out of me until I cry out in near pain.

And then he stops, his cock straining toward me, angry and frustrated.

*I'm sorry.*

"I knew your first time would be fast...but wow, William, that was amazingly quick," he begins, and I close my eyes in embarrassment. He has to know now that I can't help it.

"Open your eyes," Lex says sharply, and they snap open. He reaches up and tenderly touches my cheek.

"I wasn't making fun. I was being honest. It was amazing. That was fucking perfect," he says softly. "I feel so very flattered that I could make you feel that good. Your first time was exactly as it should have been."

I blink back the sting in my eyes and then let out a low grunt when he lifts up and I slip out of him.

Lex kisses me gently, tenderly, as if we have all the time in the world.

And we do. We have so much time.

When our mouths finally part, he stares down at me, his lips swollen and used.

"Now suck my dick, William, so we can go to sleep."

So I do.

# CHAPTER ELEVEN

**WILLIAM**

"Morning, sunshine," Lex says, his lips moving down my back. Right to the plug still lodged up my ass. Yes, I left it in there. I plan on wearing it inside of me as often as I can so that Lex can just slide right on in.

"We need to take Brenda to her doctor's appointment," Lex says, biting down on my ass lightly.

Well, he isn't motivating me to hurry. No, I want to lay here all day and let him run his lips across my skin.

"Why do you taste so good?" he asks, licking up my spine. "I'm a cannibal now."

I huff a laugh and reach over to grab my phone, blinking at the time.

"We have two hours before we have to leave, Lex."

"Yes, well, I don't want to be late," he says, his mouth now at my neck, his teeth scraping against my jugular. "And I'd like to mess around in the shower with you first. Maybe let you inside of me again. Build up your stamina."

He presses on the plug with his hand, moving it a little and I groan at the sensation.

"Will you practice some more with me, William?" he asks.

"Yes," I breathe, pushing myself up without protest and following him into the shower.

When he turns, bending slightly and placing his hands on the shower wall, I don't even hesitate. I just plunge right inside.

————

"So, you lasted like two seconds longer in the shower than you did last night," Lex says as he pulls on a pair of purple lace panties, and my cheeks burn red because yeah, I didn't last long at all. I'm not sure I ever will with him. "So, I think we need to practice *a lot* more. How about twice a day? How does that sound?"

I swallow and nod as I pull on my boxers, feeling slightly empty, because Lex took the plug out in the shower, and I feel the absence of it acutely.

"I think for that to work, you should plan on sleeping over most nights," he states, and my attention is diverted.

I meet his stare and bite my cheek. "Are you asking me to move in?"

Lex's eye twitches and he pulls his lip ring between his teeth. "No, of course not." And then he pauses and sighs. "Maybe, for a short time. We will call this a temporary arrangement. I want easy access to you, William. It's convenient for the both of us."

"Yeah. Okay," I say, feeling excitement bubbling inside of

me because this means I'll get to see him every day, every night, and basically, whenever I want.

Lex moves toward me and slants his mouth over mine, kissing me deeply.

"Good, now let's move. Brenda is waiting for us and I have shit to discuss with her doctor."

We dress hastily and make it to Brenda's place in record time.

And of course, she's delighted to see us arrive together.

"Oh, did you pick him up on your way, Lex?" she asks, and he rolls his eyes.

"Your dear William spent the night," he explains and my cheeks heat at the confession. Now my grandma knows for sure that I'm having sex with Lex, and I'm not sure I want her to know that.

Not that she can blame me for falling into temptation. I mean, just look at him. He's just made for sin.

I take him in—his long legs and torso, the sexy tattoos on his arms, his gorgeous face, and wild hair. I want to skip this doctor's appointment and fuck him again. Who knew sex could feel that good?

"Oh yes. Wonderful," she says with a bright smile, clasping her hands together. "I knew it. I knew it."

"No need to brag, Bren," he says. "You were right, we were wrong. Your grandson is delightful and delicious and I can't get enough."

*Oh my god, Lex, do not tell her that.*

But my grandma just claps her hands and links her arm with his, letting him lead her out of the facility. She's happy it's happening after months of her prattling on about him. She is probably congratulating herself on playing matchmaker.

I laugh to myself as we exit, but it's soon snuffed out when

I see the man behind the counter blushing and eyeing Lex, and Lex throws him a flirty smile and a wink. Suddenly, I feel a little sick because what the hell was that?

Has he fucked this guy? I mean, he's handsome, probably more so than me, and probably lasts longer in bed than I do. It's embarrassing now that I think about it. Seconds. I last seconds. That guy lasts at least a minute. Maybe more.

My spirits sink as we arrive at the car and Lex patiently helps Brenda into the backseat. I just sit in the passenger seat, watching it all, mulling that small interaction over and over in my head. I know I shouldn't be comparing myself to anyone else because of course Lex has fucked other people.

I mean, I met Emery, but still, it grates on my nerves.

I want to be his only one.

"Why the frown, love?" Lex says softly as he starts up the car and backs out of the parking spot.

I glance back at my grandma and see her watching us carefully. Oh, she knows. She pretends not to, but she fucking *knows*.

"Nothing," I reply and turn my gaze out the window, my eyes squinting a bit from the bright sun reflecting off the cars in the lot.

"No, something is wrong," he says softly again, and I clench my hands in my lap as he moves onto the street, driving us to the doctor's. I had put the address in his phone and turned on the GPS so he knows exactly where to go.

"Don't mind me," my grandma says happily, interrupting our softly spoken conversation. "I can't really hear you. Much."

Lex laughs. "I think she pretends her hearing is worse than it is so people talk shit in front of her."

Oh, I believe it. She's been doing that for years. I learned my lesson the hard way. Now I never underestimate her.

Lex lowers his voice to an almost inaudible level and whispers, "Tell me, William."

I eye him and see the twitch of his eye, the small tell that he's bothered by this, by how upset I am.

So, I force myself to ask, "Have you had sex with that guy back there?"

Lex's head tilts and he arches an eyebrow at me.

"Ben?" he asks.

"Oh, Ben," my grandma says. "Such a lovely boy. Very cute too."

I sigh and turn my head away because yes, he did seem lovely. And cute.

Fuck.

But before I can get too into my head about it, Lex reaches over and holds my hand.

"No," he says. "Never. I mean, I'm sure he wants me, but he's not my type. You're what I want. Just you."

His reassurance soothes my irritated, slightly bruised heart and I squeeze his hand. We hold onto each other until we are forced to part to get out of the car.

"Oh, yes, I know this place," Lex says with a wide smile, moving to help my grandma out and then walking her to the entrance. I would offer to help but he seems to enjoy doing it all himself. I don't even think he would let me help if I tried. He's just so patient and gentle with her that my heart squeezes in my chest. How I ever thought that he was after her money is beyond me. I can see how much he loves her in the way he cares for her.

I shouldn't have ever doubted it.

As soon as we enter the small doctor's office, I see a young woman behind the counter smacking her purple lips around some gum. I take in her pink hair and her low-cut top. God, we just changed providers and this is who I picked?

As soon as the girl's eyes land on Lex she rolls her eyes.

"Lex-motherfucking-ton," she chirps, the clacking on the computer stopping abruptly. "You've been ignoring my texts, asshole."

I glance around the waiting room and see that no one is bothered by her language and then laugh softly. Of course this is a friend of Lex's. We couldn't be more different if we tried. The few friends I have are boring and don't have pink hair or purple lipstick. They wear loafers and pants from Walmart.

Lex holds up a finger, walks my grandma over to a chair, and sits her down before striding back to the counter and leaning against it.

"Yes, Amanda, as you can see, I've been busy. With *impor-tant* things."

He eyes me and I shift on my feet. Because yes, he's been educating me on a lot of things. It has been very, very important and hard work.

"Nothing is more important than me," she says darkly and then folds her arms across her chest. "I expect bribes to get back into my good graces," she tells him.

"You and Diablo just think I'm exploitable, don't you?"

"Yes, we do. And you cave every time."

Lex narrows his eyes at her and then sighs. "Fine, just tell Ellie-Belly we're here. Brenda gets tired if she has to wait too long."

"Fine," she mutters and then diverts her gaze to the computer.

I guess the conversation is over then. What a mind fuck.

"Who is Ellie-Belly?" I ask as he pulls me toward where Brenda is sitting.

"A friend of mine," he explains as we find an open seat.

But instead of letting me sit on the chair next to him, he sits down and pulls me onto his lap.

This is ridiculous because I'm a grown man, not a child, but still, I fucking love it. The only problem is, now that I am on top of him, my dick is hard. I shouldn't be surprised, I really shouldn't, but I am. Because this is absolutely absurd. My cock is becoming a national monument at this point.

His hands move around my stomach and I sigh contentedly and instead of giving myself some much-needed space, I just sink back against him and come to terms with the fact that I am a goner for this man.

Brenda seems delighted at the sight of me on top of Lex and pretends not to stare, but I can feel her eyes on us. She's planning our wedding in her head. I will hear about this for months to come.

"How does your grandson smell like candy, Bren," Lex suddenly asks. "Was he like this as a child?"

"Oh yes. He was such a sweet baby," she explains, and I make a face at her because I wasn't really that sweet. I was just scared and mostly lonely.

Lex tucks his nose into my neck and inhales and my entire body flames in response.

"Yes, so fucking sweet." Then he whispers in my ear. "I wonder if your ass tastes as good."

I turn quickly on his lap to hide my erection because that thought hadn't even crossed my mind, and now it has, several times in just the past few seconds.

Lex shudders behind me, obviously thinking about it as well, and nips at my earlobe. I almost beg him to stop when suddenly the office door opens and a dark-haired man in a white lab coat and black-framed glasses steps through.

"Lex," the man, who I can only assume is the doctor by his attire, says with a loud sigh. "Of course it's you. I couldn't make this up if I tried."

Lex squeezes me tightly and then gently shoves me off his lap. He stands and helps Brenda out of her seat, leaving me to try and figure out how to hide the boner tenting the front of my pants.

It's too late though, because the woman on the other end of the room has already seen it and so has Amanda at the reception counter. The unknown woman has the decency to look away, but Amanda narrows her eyes at it, blowing a large bubble with her gum.

She holds up her finger and thumb about an inch apart and squints at it.

Is she insinuating that my dick is small?

Who the hell is this woman?

She's pure evil.

I reach down and adjust myself as best as I can, trying to ignore her stare, before following the doctor through the door and into the exam room.

I am mortified, absolutely disgusted with myself for putting on such a pornographic show, but my dick doesn't seem to give a fuck because it hasn't gone down at all.

It's reaching out toward Lex with desperation. Not that he notices. No, he's talking softly to the doctor and helping Brenda onto the examination table.

"I understand your concerns," the man says. "I'll take a look. Would you mind stepping out for a moment?"

Lex hesitates for a moment, about to protest, but then he takes my hand and leads me into the hallway. He runs a hand through his hair and then starts pacing back and forth, pulling his lip ring into his mouth over and over.

"I forgot to mention a few things to Ellie. I don't want to forget to tell him," he says, sounding a little breathless.

"Hey," I say, reaching out and stopping him, tugging him against me. "Hey, it's fine."

"Hell," he mutters, wrapping his arms around me and slumping against me. "I just want to know what they're discussing. Brenda downplays shit all the time. She will probably joke about this and it's not fucking funny."

"She's fine, Lex," I tell him. "She's just old."

"Stop saying that," he grumbles, and yet, he still tucks his face into my neck and inhales deeply. "I know that. I know it. I don't need to be reminded."

I thread my fingers through his soft hair and just hold him against me until the door opens and the doctor walks out.

Lex snaps upright and points at the doctor. "Oh, thank god. You took your sweet time, Elliot."

The doctor looks at me and a small smirk pulls up the corner of his mouth.

"Oh, so you're using my full name now," the doctor says.

"Yes, Ellie-Belly, I am. I mean business. Now tell us, what's up."

Elliot eyes me. "You're her grandson?"

I nod and Lex stiffens beside me, and I reach out and thread my fingers with his. He doesn't need to be reminded that he's not.

"Well, she's fine. Everything looks good and the lab work that she had done earlier this month is within normal limits."

Lex waves a hand in the air. "Yes, we know that, but she's tired all the time. Always falling asleep."

"Yes, well, she's—"

"Do not fucking say it," Lex mutters, and Elliot narrows his eyes at him. "I hear it all the fucking time."

Elliot eyes our hands and then sighs loudly. "Well, she is, Lex. But she's fine. There is nothing to be worried about. I'll see her again in a few months, or sooner if anything comes up."

Lex sags in relief and then leans toward Elliot. "You're telling me the truth, right? Because you know what I did for you...you *owe* me."

Elliot's cheeks darken and he folds his arms across his chest.

"Yes, I do know and yes, I am telling you the truth."

Lex examines him closely for a moment and then lets go of my hand, marching into the room and leaving me with the doctor.

He eyes me and then says, "Really, out of all the people I imagined Lex with, it was not someone like you."

My eyebrows meet at that, and my mouth opens to protest because yes, we are different, but we work just fine. But before I can utter a single word, he interrupts me.

"It's just an odd pairing, that's all I'm saying, but who am I to talk?"

When I don't respond he just sighs. "Never mind. Do you have any other concerns or questions?"

I shake my head and then stop suddenly. "Actually, yes, I do."

Then I feel my face flush to epic proportions because really, is this my life right now?

"I have a question about *me*, actually."

Elliot's eyebrow rises, and I clear my throat, stalling because I don't know how to word it.

"Any day now," Elliot mutters.

I just decide to go for it before my grandma makes an appearance. She doesn't need to hear this.

"Ever since meeting Lex, my...." I gesture to my crotch. "It's up all the time," I whisper, trying to be discreet.

Elliot looks at me and then looks at my crotch. "It's called *attraction*."

I feel my skin nearly melt off my body and then shake my head. "There's nothing I can do?"

"Unfortunately, no. You're going to have to just suffer through."

"But it's bothersome. When I say all the time, I mean *all the time*."

He purses his lips and adjusts his glasses.

"Then I suggest you stay away from Lex if he's the one causing this."

My head lurches back. "Impossible."

"Then you're doomed. There is no hope left," he says with a small smirk.

Is he deriving pleasure from this? What an asshole.

The exam door opens, and I eyeball Lex who is helping my grandma cross the hallway and I feel my heart clench.

"I am doomed," I mutter, adjusting my dick in my pants once more.

There's nothing to be done, it seems.

I am stuck with a hard dick for life.

I have accepted my fate.

# CHAPTER TWELVE

## LEX

"Okay," I say, trying to get the ladies to listen to me. They're talking over me though and I am growing exasperated. They pretend not to hear me with their hearing aids, but it's all a lie. I know they can. I don't even know if they really need hearing aids, to be honest.

These women have the hearing range of motherfucking hawks when they want to.

"Hello?" I say a little louder, waving my hands a little to try and get their attention. But no one bats an eye at me.

I glance over and see William smiling at the whole situation and I roll my eyes. He's unhelpful as usual. But still just as delicious.

You will apologize, William, once I get my tongue up your ass. You'll beg me for forgiveness.

I move in front of the three of them chatting happily on the couch and place my hands on my hips, narrowing my eyes at them. But no one is paying any attention to me. Not until William moves up to my side and runs his hand across my stomach.

Their banter slows and finally, all of their eyes are on us.

Oh, these nosy bitches. Always harping on us. *When is the wedding? Can I be in the wedding party?*

They just skipped over the boyfriend part entirely and have the two of us engaged. They've already started a Honeyfund for us, for fuck's sake.

I had to look that shit up when Martha mentioned it. I had no idea what it meant. Sounded a little kinky. But it turns out, they're planning our honeymoon to Tahiti.

I've known William for two weeks. They're out of their minds.

Not so fast, ladies. Give me at least a month.

"Oh, Lex," Martha says with a sly smile. "So sorry. Were you talking to us?"

I point my finger at her as I lean into William. He smells like coconuts.

"I was, actually, and you know it. You only just paid attention because William is here now, and he looks edible."

I peek over at him, seeing his red cheeks, and smirk a little.

Nothing has changed. He still turns the color of bubblegum every time I look at him.

That will never get old.

Martha smirks at me and the corners of my mouth turn up in a smile. These mischievous ladies. Giving me hell. I probably deserve it. Karma and all that shit.

"What's so important that you just had to interrupt us?" Vikki asks.

I narrow my eyes at her, and she blows me a kiss. I

ignore it, even though my heart swells from the gesture. I never had parents who did things like this. I don't remember one affectionate touch. To be honest, I don't know why my mother even had me. I was a nuisance, a bother, something she was saddled with. She spent more time yelling at me, throwing things at me, and hurting me than anything else. And then there were days she'd just flat-out ignore me.

I never knew this kind of normalcy until I met these women.

These goofy signs of affection have taken some getting used to but now I wish I'd never had to go without them.

"Okay, so I know you all have been nagging me to bring you to get tattoos..." They all start talking once more and I have to wait for them to quiet down. But my ear catches something Brenda is saying, and I frown.

"Absolutely not, Bren. You will be getting one over my dead body and William agrees. Right?"

Brenda eyes her grandson and he nods his head, his hand snaking around my back and settling on my ass.

You filthy man. And in front of your grandma too.

"I agree with Lex," he says, squeezing my cheek gently.

Oh, I am going to get him back for this later. Fucking around with William is just as exciting as the first time. Every time.

Brenda's eyes sparkle and I lean over and press a kiss to his cheek. Hmm, that's not enough. I grab onto his jaw and tilt his face toward mine, pressing my lips to his.

I'd kiss him deeper, just stick my tongue inside of him, but we have onlookers.

They're oddly quiet, whispering to each other.

Plotting, I'm sure.

"I'm thinking blue and red for the wedding colors," Vikki says and Martha snorts.

"What the hell is that about? Are you thinking of Captain America? Are we trying to be patriotic?"

"I didn't say white too!" Vikki quips.

"I think blue and purple," Brenda says softly. "Blue for William, something to match his eyes. And purple for Lex because he just shines."

Well, now my eyeballs are watering. Fuck this.

William rests his head on my shoulder.

"That sounds good, grandma."

Oh, so he's on board all of a sudden? He hasn't said a word to me about it since they brought it up a few days ago and now he's giving them the green light?

"Who said I'd marry you?" I ask, arching an eyebrow at him.

He glances up at me, those blue eyes of his so endearing, and I just melt.

"Fine. If you insist. We will discuss details later."

Brenda claps her hands together and then leans back a little on the couch, while Martha and Vikki bicker over table settings and the venue.

My god, they are just as bad as Emery. I need to bring him into the fold. He'd fit in seamlessly. Perhaps he can help with the wedding planning. We'd end up on a rocket ship to Mars if that were the case.

"Hey!" I shout and all of their heads swivel to me. "Stop getting me off track. I have a surprise. Uma and Rhea are coming to do henna tattoos in five minutes so get your shit together."

"What the hell is a henna tattoo?" Martha asks.

I pull out my phone and pull up a picture, showing it to

them. They ooh and ahh over it for a long minute and then Brenda blinks up at me, her head tilted slightly.

"What made you do this?"

"I said no tattoos and I mean it. So, this is a compromise," I tell them and peek over at William who is just watching me carefully.

He turns his head and says gently, "Yes. We compromise in this family."

They, of course, listen to him, bobbing their heads in agreement, giving him none of the shit they give me most days.

But I don't care at the moment because my heart is exploding in my chest. He just said I was a part of this family.

I've never had one of those before.

Fuck, this man.

I am going to make him come so hard tonight.

"You did that on purpose," I whisper to him, and he smiles softly at me.

"Yes, but only because it's true."

Ugh, he is making me feel things that I don't know if I can handle. I'm already a bit of a mess. Spending every day and night with William is just doing things to my heart. Waking up next to him, falling asleep in his arms...

I didn't know living with someone like this could make me so happy.

I didn't know I needed it until now.

A knock on the door has me pulling away from William's embrace to answer it. Good thing too. My eyes were stinging. I'm not sure I should let myself cry in front of the ladies. Or William.

What would he think of me?

When I pull the door open, two young women are

standing there, one with a travel case in her hand.

"Are you Lex?" the taller one asks, and I nod.

"Come on in," I say. "You can set up in the living room."

They follow me to where the ladies are and begin setting up their equipment. I can see them sneaking peaks at William. I don't blame them one bit. He's so damn handsome and sweet. But he's mine. So without hesitation, I grab onto William's hand, pulling him toward a free chair. I push him down onto it and crawl onto his lap, staking my claim. I have turned into a caveman...one with impeccable style, but still. Mine. He's mine.

And apparently, I'm his because he snakes his hands around my stomach, one sneaking up underneath my shirt, playing with my belly button piercing. He doesn't even seem to notice the beautiful women in the room, his eyes are only on me.

"They're so excited," he says, pressing a kiss to my neck and then licking at it gently. I glance over to see Brenda with a big grin on her face, her arm outstretched, and one of the henna tattoo artists starting to paint a design onto her skin. "This was a good idea."

I wiggle my ass against him. "I know, William. You can thank me later."

———

"They loved it," I say as we walk out of the facility, hand in hand. I can see Ben looking at the two of us, his eyes a little sad.

I feel bad. Kind of.

He'll find his William.

It will be so worth the wait.

"They did. You did good, Lexington."

I lean into him and bask in his praise. Because hell yes, I did. After the tattoos were complete, the ladies *oohed* and *aahed* over them, comparing the intricate designs on their arms and hands to each other's.

I think their blood lust for tattoos has been sated. For a while, at least. Now I can at least put the worry of an infection overtaking one of them out of my mind.

Thank fuck.

When we get to William's ridiculous sports car, I lean against it and pull him into me. The sun is still unbearably hot as it beats down on us, but I still can't help myself. I blame him for being so tempting. I'd walk through fire to get to him.

"You should have let me drive you here," I say, slanting my mouth over his and slipping my tongue into his mouth.

He kisses me fervently for a moment and then pulls away. "I know, but I had to go home and grab some more clothes."

I arch an eyebrow and William leans toward me, his lips ghosting across my jaw.

"Why bother? You always end up naked anyways," I groan, wondering if William would let me fuck him in the back of my car. We'd never fit in the back of his. Ridiculous, stupid car.

I hate how sexy it is.

William groans a little, arching his hips against me and I smirk. Always so eager.

Soon I'll be inside of him. Very soon if he's been wearing his plug like he's supposed to.

Right now, I'm content with letting him fuck me. And he's content to do it too. He wants inside of me all the time. Begs for it.

Like this morning.

I woke to him watching me intently, his gaze hot and needy. Just from the look on his face, I knew what he wanted.

So I rolled over onto my stomach, crossed my arms under my head, and spread my legs a little.

He'd scrambled over eagerly, spreading my cheeks, lubing me up, and slipping inside.

It was a fantastic way to spend my morning, stretched wide open for him.

I love how he pants and groans as he comes. He lasts longer and longer each time.

He's up to a minute now.

I'm hoping by the end of the year, he can last five. Baby steps and all that.

"Let's go home, fuck around, eat something, and just lounge around. I have something I need to do for a friend of mine."

William presses his overheated forehead against my shoulder and inhales deeply.

"Okay, yeah. Sounds good."

"And I'll make some more space for you in the closet."

His eyes widen. "But I already took a drawer."

"I'm very, very accommodating."

"You are," he says, running a hand up my chest and making me shake with need. If I knew I wouldn't get arrested, I'd bend over right here for him.

My glovebox has all sorts of things inside of it, like lube. A whole container of it for emergencies like this.

"Meet me at home," I tell him and kiss him again.

It takes another five minutes to peel ourselves away and then he's following me back to my place. When William steps out of his car, I link my hand with his and tug him quickly into the apartment.

I want him naked. I want to run my hands along his body. Then I want to kiss him endlessly and afterward just let him hold me.

Or I can hold him.

I just want us to hold onto each other.

How did I get this obsessed in such a short time when my entire life I didn't need this intimacy, didn't crave it?

I don't know how it happened. All I know is that I am now and there's no going back.

I. Am. Obsessed.

William is all I can think about. I even dream about him.

As soon as the door shuts behind us, I'm grabbing onto his shirt, unbuttoning it, wanting my hands on his skin.

I push it off his shoulders and bite down on his collarbone.

"Delicious," I mutter against him. "How about I put that plug in you...."

"Yes," he moans.

"And make you wear it while I finish up some stuff."

"You're going to make me wait?" he asks, looking up at me, his cheeks red, his lips swollen from biting on them.

"Mhmm, I have a project that cannot wait. So come on. Chop, chop."

My hand grabs onto his and I pull him into the room.

"Pants off."

William tugs them down roughly and then bends over, completely, deliciously naked, while I grab the plug and the lube.

It goes in easier than I expect, and when it's seated neatly inside of him, I run my hand over it.

"Good. Very nice," I say and then take a step back, adjusting myself. Because I am very tempted right now.

But I have a deadline.

Diablo is not going to be happy. I put off this project, too consumed with William, and he's going to come to collect.

"Now come sit near me while I work," I tell him and pull out the chair I'd bought for him a few days ago.

He's spent very little time sitting in it. Mostly he's on my lap, but while I paint, I need space to move and focus. I can't focus when he's on me.

I watch as he sits down, a gasp escaping his mouth and I smirk.

Yes, William, that can't be comfortable.

But still, I let him writhe a bit in his seat, enjoying the view as I take out my tools and begin painting the minis Diablo gave me.

"So, tell me, what got you into painting these?" William asks, his attempt to distract himself is so damn cute.

"Well, I've always liked gaming and a few years ago my friend Diablo brought me to a game store where we played a board game with these miniatures. I realized that while I like the game, I like the idea of painting the figurines more."

"You seem very good at it," he says.

"I am good at a lot of things, as you well know."

He nods, biting down on his bottom lip, his eyes roving over me and for a moment. I smirk at him and then wrench my eyes away so I can focus.

I manage for quite a while until William starts whimpering.

"For god's sake, what is going on?" I say, turning my head, my paintbrush in my hand.

"Shit. Sorry."

I set my paintbrush down and swivel my chair toward him. "Do you need to go to the bed? If so, that's fine."

William nods and moves over to it, lying down on his

stomach.

I make an honest effort to focus on my project, but I can see him out of the corner of my eye slowly humping the mattress.

Well, that's no fair. The bed is having all the fun and I'm sitting over here doing something that pales in comparison.

I never was one for self-control.

I set the figurine down.

It can wait. William, however, cannot, it seems. I know how eager his dick is. He will be coming on my sheets in a matter of minutes if I don't get control of this situation immediately.

I move toward him and he stares up at me, desperation lingering in his eyes.

"So impatient," I say, running a finger down his back. "Stop doing that."

He stills and I lean down pressing my mouth to his.

"Now, I have work to do and you're distracting me, so let's take care of this first. Turn over."

William shakes his head. "No."

My eyebrows rise at that. "Excuse me? Did you just tell me no?"

He nods once. "I want you. Inside of me."

My body stiffens at that because *good lord*. I'd been wanting it for days but didn't want to rush him.

"I don't know if you're—"

"I'm ready," he says. "So ready."

"You sure, love?" I ask softly because I want his first time to be good, really good. I want him to remember it for years to come. I want him to dream about this moment, here, with me.

"Yeah."

I press down on the plug and then slowly start to work it out of him. Shit, it's a snug fit. It really has a good grip. It doesn't help that he's fucking back against it like a slut.

"William Bernard," I mutter. "Stop that."

He doesn't stop. It's a miracle I manage to dislodge it from his ass. When I finally do, he's groaning, his hole ready and waiting for me. I take a nice long lingering look.

Take a good look, dick, this is your home now.

"Turn over, love. I want to see your gorgeous face while I fuck you for the first time. I want to watch it all." I smack his ass cheek and then move to the bathroom to toss the plug into the sink.

When I return, William is on his back, his legs lifted to his chest, two of his fingers up his ass. I can hear it from where I stand, the slick slide of him fucking himself.

"Stop that," I say, striding toward him and swatting at his hand. "My god, you're going to come without me."

But he doesn't listen. He just keeps fucking himself. If he finishes before I can get in there, I'm going to be so mad.

I tug on his hand and his fingers slip out reluctantly.

"Bad William," I chastise, stripping out of my clothes. He watches me peel my jeans off, his hand clasped tightly around the base of his dick. Oh, always so eager and ready to blow.

I reach for the lube and slick up my dick. William is scooting closer and closer, his ass trying to impale itself on my cock.

"So fucking impatient," I mutter with a small grin.

My smile disappears though when I stick the tip of my dick right at his hole with a trembling hand because hell, I'm excited. It's been so long since I've been inside of someone. Years, really. Emery never let me do this, and the man before him didn't either.

Come to think of it, I rarely ever top.

And I want to top. At least fifty percent of the time.

"Ready?" I ask, but William doesn't even answer. He just grabs onto my hips and yanks me forward and my cock is sucked right inside of his tight, warm hole.

"Motherfucker," I groan, buried balls deep inside of him. "What was that? *What the fuck was that?*" I gasp, feeling how snug he is around me.

William claws at my back, his mouth open in a gasp because his hole just sucked up my dick like a vacuum inhaling a Cheerio.

"Lexington," he groans and the way he says my name, like a prayer, makes my entire body clench with need.

"You better not come, William. I am not done with you yet," I say, my entire body vibrating with pent-up lust.

I mean, I probably won't last long either, but I want at least a few thrusts thrown in there for good measure. I have standards and expectations for myself.

I should make another award for myself if I manage to last longer than a minute.

I pull back, sliding out of him before thrusting forward and William cries out, his skin red and flushed.

"Shit," I say, his ass gripping me like a vise. My god, he's tight.

I let my cock drag out of him again before stuffing him full and our entire bodies slide up the bed an inch from the force of it.

"Goddamn you," I grumble. This feels entirely too good, and William seems to think so too because his dick is leaking profusely and he's groaning so loud I know the neighbors can hear.

They will congratulate me when they see me.

"More!" he cries, and that just snaps something inside of me. I pound into him, trying my best to keep it together, but he feels too good, smells too good. I lean down and lick a stripe up his neck. He tastes good too, like sex and candy.

He's calling out my name, begging me for release and my rhythm falters. I'm so fucking close.

"Come first," I pant, and his hand starts frantically jerking himself off.

It only takes a second and then he's gushing onto his chest, his ass clamping around me, over and over, his orgasm going on for ages. My balls draw up and I press firmly into him, unloading my cum as far up into him as I can.

When the waves of pleasure finally stop, I lower my trembling body on top of him and his arms move around my back, stroking me gently.

"That was very short. I apologize," I mutter, pressing my lips to the side of his neck. "Next time will be better."

William huffs a small laugh. "No. It was perfect."

"It's just been a while since my dick's been aggressively hoovered by an asshole."

He chuckles softly and squeezes me tighter to his chest. "It wanted you inside of me. It couldn't wait."

"Well, next time I *will* last longer, I *promise*," I say, feeling the slickness of his release between our bodies. "But for now, let's clean up. How does your ass feel?"

He clenches his hole around me, and I huff at the sensation.

"Damn you," I mutter, gently pulling out of him.

"It feels good...*used*. I like it," he says as I help him stand up.

I lead him into the bathroom, pushing against his back,

bending him over, and I spread his cheeks to look at his swollen, wet hole. I preen.

I did that.

I press against it gently and it puckers against my finger.

"I'm going to clean you up."

"I can do it," he protests, but he doesn't move. I take care to wipe him up as best I can, and then I make sure to put him in some pants. Diablo is coming over in an hour and I haven't finished the miniatures I owe him. William is way too distracting when naked. I just want to stare at him, like he's some piece of fine art. I'd hang him up on my wall and admire him. Creepy? Yes. But do I fucking care? No. Not in the least.

"Can we watch it?" he asks me as he pulls on a pair of athletic shorts.

I turn to look at him and I don't know why I'm surprised. I shouldn't be, filthy fucker.

"Yes, of course. Tonight, before bed. You can see your first time."

Then I sink down in my chair and William sits in his, throwing his legs over mine as he leans back, his eyes closed.

I just stare at him for a moment...just take a really long look at *my* William.

"Are you staring at me?" he asks, peeking open an eye and catching me.

I flick my gaze back to my miniature and shrug. "You're hot and shirtless. I like looking at your nipples."

He smiles gently and sighs. "Get your work done so I can hold you."

Gah, I want to be held too. Emery will just die if he ever finds out. I turn my attention back to my paints and do my best to finish before Diablo shows up, but I wasted too much time playing in William's ass. Before I know it, there's banging on my door.

"Shit," I mutter. "He's always fucking late and *now* he decides to be on time?"

William flings his legs off of mine and stands up.

"Want me to get it?" he asks, making his way over to the front door. Before I even have time to warn him, or to tell him to cover up that sexy, freckled chest of his, I hear, "Who the fuck are you? Are you Lex's?"

I round the corner and see William nodding in response. Moving toward him, I narrow my eyes at Diablo who is blatantly checking William out. I mean, he's not even discrete about it. His eyes are currently stuck on William's groin.

"Eyes in appropriate places, Diablo," I snark and Diablo's gaze snaps to mine.

"They're thin shorts. They're made for gawking."

"Well, show a little respect."

Diablo narrows his eyes at me as Skylar lumbers in behind him, towering over him, and I sigh. Because of course he's here. Apparently, things haven't been resolved with the family yet. It must be very, very serious.

"Well, are you going to be rude or introduce us?" Diablo asks, like he gives a flying fuck about politeness.

"Diablo, this is William. He's mine. You can't have him," I say saucily. "Not that he'd want you. You have crumbs on your shirt."

Diablo folds his arms across his chest and purses his lips. "You are entirely too rude. Don't you think so, Skylar?"

But Skylar is too busy staring at William to answer.

Well fuck me sideways, this is getting a little ridiculous. No one else should be looking at him like he's edible. That's reserved for me.

"Go put a shirt on," I hiss at him, finally at my wit's end, but William just raises his brow and cocks his head at me. The movement reminds me so much of Brenda that a loud, awkward laugh escapes me.

"My gods, William. You are doing this on purpose, aren't you? To torment me? Did Brenda put you up to this?"

"Who the fuck is Brenda?" Diablo asks, moving toward my kitchen and rummaging through my cabinets.

The nosy, hungry fucker. He's like a bear. A tiny one. He just constantly rummages around for food. Hmm, maybe he's more like a raccoon.

He always makes out with some of my shit before he leaves. Diablo, the trash panda. He's endearing in an altogether annoying way.

"These crackers are stale," Diablo says, around a mouthful of food, a box in his hand. "Disgusting." He takes another heaping handful anyways, shoving more between his cheeks like a chipmunk and I roll my eyes. Because really, no one would ever guess this man was raised by millionaire mobsters.

He is utterly ridiculous.

"Where is my shit?" he says, pulling out a carton of milk and gulping it down. He doesn't even get a glass, just drinks it straight from the container. Gross. "I need it for tomorrow."

"Well," I begin as I feel William lean up against me, his hands running across my skin, and I light up, literally. My entire body has awoken and it's remembering what it was like to be inside of him. "It's not done yet, but I can finish up in an hour. By all means, eat some more of my stuff. You haven't ravaged the pantry yet."

"I have deadlines, Lex," Diablo grumbles.

"Well, I had more important shit to do."

"I'm charging you interest."

"Fine. Go sit, Skylar," Diablo says, and I watch as Skylar lowers his body onto the couch, the entire thing almost bowing under his weight.

Yes, he can't help that he's gigantic, but I won't tolerate disrespect for my things. I paid a lot of money for that couch and now there are memories of William attached to it. It's become quite sentimental.

I point a finger at Skylar. "If you break it, you buy it."

He just stares at me and then moves his eyes to William.

Oh my fucking god. *Enough*.

"Do not look at him, Skylar. Because I will end you."

He doesn't look convinced. Well, what the fuck ever. I can be just as scary as Diablo. I just don't work as fast as him. But I can make him disappear. It would take a while to hack that ginormous body up, but I could do it.

Grabbing William's arm, I pull him into the bedroom. My hands press on his shoulders, pushing him down onto his chair.

I waggle my finger in front of his face. "Do not move."

He leans back and I see his half-hard cock pressing against his shorts. My eyebrows meet as I lean into him.

"You were being very flirty out there."

A small smile turns the corners of his lips up. "I didn't say a word."

"You flirted by existing. It's a thing you do."

"Says the biggest flirt on earth."

I bend down and press my lips to his sassy mouth before pulling away.

"Just stay away from the two of them, especially the sexy ogre out there, and let me work. Do not, I repeat, do not go out there."

And thank god, he doesn't fight me. He just closes his eyes

and props his legs on mine once more. In the other room, I can hear Diablo muttering things to Skylar and I can hear Skylar's gruff voice as Diablo continues to rummage around my place.

I'll check my cameras later to see what he took and either tack it onto his bill or seek revenge.

I manage to finish in record time and when I emerge an hour later, I see all the cabinets in my kitchen open and Diablo perched on the couch nearest Skylar texting furiously on his phone.

"Done," I say, presenting him with the two figurines I owe him.

As Diablo inspects my work, William moves up behind me and slides his hands around my waist. I don't think I'll ever grow tired of him touching me. And to think just a few weeks ago I was only concerned with ridding myself of him.

My, how the tides have shifted.

"Good work," Diablo says, cupping both minis in his hand. "I think we're even now."

My fingers link with William's as I lean back slightly, resting my head on his shoulder.

"Good. Now, you all can leave. I have things to do," I say, wanting them to just shoo the fuck away.

Diablo narrows his eyes at me and then gestures for Skylar to get up off the couch. The thing creaks and groans in relief.

The two of them make their way out of the apartment, leaving William and me alone.

I turn my head, my lips brushing against his cheek.

"So sorry about that, but now you're all mine. Ready to watch your first time on repeat?" I ask as his hand travels down to my crotch, cupping me gently.

"Fuck yeah."

# CHAPTER THIRTEEN

**WILLIAM**

The buzzing of my phone has me peeling my eyelids back. Ugh, my entire body aches. Rightfully so because after watching the recording of my first time on Lex's computer, we fucked again, this time with me riding him right in his computer chair.

My ass is sore but I wouldn't change a thing. I like bottoming for Lex. I prefer it actually. I want to do it this way forever and always, as long as we both shall live.

My phone buzzes aggressively against the end table and I reach out for it. Lex tucks himself further into me, his warm breath puffing against my neck.

"Hello?" I say groggily into the phone as Lex's hard cock ruts against my ass. Hmm, I could probably do it again, if he lubes up really well.

"Is this William Walker, Brenda's grandson?" an unknown voice says, and all thoughts of dick flee from my mind.

Lex stiffens behind me, obviously having heard the voice on the other end of the line, and props himself up, his eyes wide with worry.

"Yes, what is it?" I ask, reaching out and cupping his neck gently, wanting to reassure him.

"Brenda took a fall this morning on her way to grab breakfast at the dining hall..." the woman explains, but before she can continue, Lex shoots out of bed, his movements frantic and choppy as he tries to dress himself. He stumbles slightly into the wall and curses under his breath.

Fuck, I can tell he's not going to take this well.

I groan as I sit up, trying to remain more levelheaded. Because yes, I hate this, hate that she's fallen, but it's happened before. Old people do this all the time. She broke her foot two years ago getting out of bed, and right before I left for Florida, she bruised her entire right side just walking to the bathroom.

Lex wasn't there for any of it and he doesn't realize that this happens. Yes, it's okay to get upset because it sucks, but there's no point in getting panicky.

And right now, Lex is hysterical, his eyes almost wild.

"What do we need to do?" I ask, moving my focus back to the woman on the line.

"Well, the EMTs are here, and they are going to transport her to the hospital..." She rattles off the name of where she will be brought and I hang up, pushing myself out of bed and moving toward a desperate-looking Lex. His pants are unbuttoned, his shirt hanging half off his body, and his chest is heaving.

"Hey," I say, approaching him cautiously. He lets out a shattered groan when I reach out and tug his shirt fully on, letting my hand slide across his warm chest. "It's okay. Let's not worry until we get there, okay?"

He gives me a shaky nod.

"Hurry, please," he says softly. I reach up, pressing a kiss to his lips, and then I'm tugging on my clothes and being pulled out of the apartment by Lex.

"I'm driving," I say, unlocking my car because there is no way I'm letting Lex get behind the wheel as upset as he is. His eyes are glassy and he's gnawing on his bottom lip, his leg bouncing frantically.

"Fuck, I need a cigarette," he mutters, looking out the window, chewing on his thumb nail. "Shouldn't have quit. Terrible timing."

I reach over and tug his hand away from his mouth, linking my fingers with his.

"She'll be okay."

"How do you know?" he asks with a sniffle, his eye twitching.

"She fell two years ago. She was just hurt and in pain, but she was okay."

He stares at me a frown on his face. "That was entirely unhelpful, William. Why on earth would you tell me that?"

A small laugh escapes me because yeah, that wasn't helpful, and his frown dips further. "Not. Funny."

I bite my bottom lip because he's just so damn precious right now. I want to tuck him away and keep him safe from any heartbreak.

I pull his hand up to my lips and press a gentle kiss to his knuckles as I pull onto the freeway.

When we arrive at Hoag Hospital twenty minutes later, Lex power walks through the parking lot and I have to jog to keep up with him.

"What if they don't let me in?" he asks, his eyes frenzied, his hand sweating in mine. "I'm not family."

"You are," I say, as we step in line at the reception desk. "You're her grandson."

Lex's breath wooshes out of him as he runs a hand across his cheek, his eyes meeting mine, glassy and wide.

"Stop it," he whispers to me, pulling me into him and pressing a kiss to my mouth. "Stop being so fucking wonderful."

I grin and I wrap my arms around him. Because no, I won't stop. I'm going to keep being wonderful because he deserves it, and above all, I hope we can keep doing what we're doing. I like waking up next to him, falling asleep in his arms, and just spending time with him.

I crave the feel of him, the taste of him, the smell of him. He is everywhere—in my body, my heart, and my fucking soul.

I don't know how it happened so fast, but it did. And I have no desire to go back to the way things were. To do so would be devastating.

When we finally make our way into my grandma's room, Lex visibly sags in relief. I told him she would be fine, but he didn't believe me. He needed to see it with his own eyes.

"Bren," he says in irritation, pulling her gaze to him. "What in the fuck did you manage to do?"

My grandma smiles at him widely, her eyes twinkling as she glances at her arm resting limply on the bed.

"They say it's just sprained."

Lex rolls his eyes and moves toward her.

"Jesus Christ. Were you running around like I told you not to? Where was your walker, huh? And what is this on your neck?"

He points to the brace around her neck, and she lets out a small, pained laugh.

"Broke my neck a little."

Lex's eyes widen and he turns to look at me, shocked. Then his head swivels back to my grandma. "How can you break it a little? That is not a thing, Bren."

"Apparently it is. I must have a superpower."

"Do not joke about this. It's not funny," he mutters, and I know he's about to lose it. I move toward him, wrapping him up in my arms. He melts into me, his hands moving up my back.

"You and William are both awful. Laughing about bad, scary shit," Lex mutters.

"I didn't laugh," I explain, but Lex just ignores me, his eyes moving around the small room.

"Where is the doctor? The service here is awful."

"I just got here a bit ago," my grandma says, moving her good arm and turning her palm up.

Lex pulls away from me and lowers himself onto the edge of the bed, his hand slipping into hers.

"Well, they should place more value on care. This is ridiculous. People could be meeting Jesus right and left in here without anyone monitoring them."

"I'm not meeting Jesus today," she says. "Not yet, at least."

He frowns deeply, his whole body stiffening.

"I'm just so happy to see you and William together. I'm glad that you have each other. It's all I've ever wanted for both of you. So when the time comes, I can die a happy woman."

Lex shakes his head.

"Do. Not. *Even.*"

I watch how my grandma looks at him with adoration in

her eyes, and how Lex handles her with such care. My chest constricts and I press against it. It aches.

"William said you fall often," Lex says suddenly.

My grandma meets my eyes and I shrug. Because what was I supposed to do? Keep it a secret? I didn't know it was one.

"Yes, well I'm old. It's a thing we do. Our legs don't work like they should."

Lex leans a little closer to her. "I got you that walker. You need to use it from now on. You are no longer allowed to keep it as a decoration. Promise me, Bren."

She squeezes his hand and tries to give another nod, but winces instead.

"I will do my best to remember."

"Your best is not good enough," Lex mutters and I let out a small chuckle.

But at the glower he sends my way, I bite it back.

"I love you, Bren," he says, turning to meet her eyes. "I mean it. Don't do reckless things...like walk around."

My grandma reaches out and runs her hand along his cheek.

"Love you too, Lex."

He just leans into her touch, reveling in it.

I press my back against the wall and watch quietly, letting them have their time. I've had Brenda all my life. I was so damn lucky. And now...now Lex can have his turn.

I want him to have this kind of love for as long as he can.

————

"The hospital rules are bullshit," Lex mutters as he buckles himself into the car. "We should be able to stay the night."

I link my hand with his as I press the button and the

motor roars to life. "She can go home tomorrow. We'll come back as soon as we can to pick her up."

Lex runs a hand down his face and sighs, obviously unhappy with the entire situation. He threw a bit of a fit moments ago when we were told visiting hours were over. At one point, he glowered at the nurse and threatened to "end her", saying he can "be very creative when it comes to disposing of bodies."

Brenda laughed it off as the nurse sent him wary glances, but in the end, it made me like him even more. I admire how protective he is of the people he loves.

And he's protective of me. Does that mean this thing between us runs just as deep for him as it does for me?

"Or you can get her alone if you want. I wouldn't mind," I offer because I know how much he appreciates her attention when her focus isn't split between the two of us. When we first met, I just assumed he was being ridiculous and juvenile, but now I understand him better. He savors the time he has alone with her, and I don't blame him.

Lex eyes me and pulls his lip ring into his mouth. He shakes his head once. "No, we can do it together."

I squeeze his hand. "I like doing things with you."

"I do too. Which is a surprise. I have been solo for so long."

"Me too, but now we have each other."

"Look, I don't do boyfriends, William," Lex says, and I feel my heart sink, because what the fuck is this thing between us then? Maybe I was wrong and he doesn't feel anything deeper for me. But then he just sighs and adds, "But I'll be yours if you want. And speaking of that, it's probably best if we made long-term plans."

"Long term?" I ask because I didn't even think about that.

I know that my grandma, Vikki, and Martha have been harping on about the two of us getting married and I just went along with it for shits and giggles. I didn't think anything of it really. The only thing that rings true at this moment is that I want him. Always.

"Yes, *long term*. I've never done that before, but the ladies are counting on us. We're up to two thousand dollars in the Honeyfund, so we should probably get married."

A nervous cough escapes my throat as I pull onto the freeway. What the hell has gotten into him? Marriage? Is he insane? I mean we joked about it the other day, but he seems scarily serious at the moment.

"Lex, we just met."

"So? When you know, you know."

"Lexington," I say sternly and he groans, throwing his head back against the headrest and staring at the roof of the car.

"Fine, no marriage yet. But soonish. Okay? I know the ladies would love planning it."

My eyes narrow because that doesn't sound like he loves me or that he even wants to marry me. I don't even know why we're having this ridiculous conversation three weeks after we met but my mouth can't stop flapping.

"So you'd marry me just to make them happy?" I ask.

He huffs and turns his head a little, watching me. "No, of course not. My parents never married, and their *friends* never sealed the deal, so it's not like I had any good examples growing up. So I never expected to do it myself. But when I think of being with you, it's not so bad."

*Not so bad*, my god, this man.

"I'm not marrying you," I mutter, feeling...annoyed by this conversation. Among other things.

To be honest, I never planned on marrying anyone either but now the first person I could see myself committed to is only considering it for my grandma's sake. Well, this is just my luck.

"Why not?" Lex asks, his tone annoyed. "Why are you saying no now? You've never said it to me before? You always just say yes. Well, except for yesterday when you wanted me to fuck you..."

"Because I will not be some kind of...pity husband."

I pull the car into a parking spot and stumble out. This conversation is dumb, and I've had some pretty stupid conversations in my life. I work in accounting after all. I stomp toward the building but Lex grabs onto my arm, stopping me in my tracks.

"You running away?" he asks and I shrug out of his hold.

"No, I'm headed to your apartment. I'm doing the opposite of running."

He huffs, "You are such a brat."

I glance over my shoulder at him and continue moving toward his place. "You love it."

His eyes grow hooded, electricity sparking between us. "Yes, I do."

When we enter his apartment, the annoyance I felt in the parking lot is still there and it's not fading nearly as fast as I want it to.

It's probably because I'm still exhausted from such a long day at the hospital. Around lunchtime I had to run to work for a bit and Jason was huffing and puffing at me like usual. I'd just ignored him, rushing through my work to get back to Lex. But I could hear him grumbling at his desk, his fan on full blast. I didn't want him to be even more stressed out because now that I think of it, he does look unhealthy and I'd feel terrible if he just keeled over, so I extended my stay in the office to help him with some stuff.

But now here I am at Lex's apartment, and we are in a sort-of fight, I think, and I'm tired and wrung out and I just want to lay down and hold him.

"You wouldn't be a pity husband," Lex says when I start to take my shirt off.

"Well, I'd feel like one after that conversation," I say, shrugging it off my shoulders and tossing it onto a chair.

He rolls his eyes and then steps into my space, his hands sliding around my bare hips, tugging me against him.

"I am *consumed* by you," he says, running one of his hands through my hair and tugging on it. "I have never felt this way about another person."

My breath leaves my body and I stare at him. "It doesn't matter anyways. It's too fast."

"Fast is the only way to live."

He presses his lips to mine, and I melt into him.

When we stumble into his room and he slips inside of me again, any lingering agitation dissipates completely.

He's right. I'll only ever say yes to him.

# CHAPTER FOURTEEN

**LEX**

I sleep better than I expected. Probably because I am half on top of William all night and for some reason, his cool, quiet demeanor just takes me down a fucking notch. I get why Emery is so enamored with August.

Sometimes us anxious people just need a calm guy to help us relax a bit.

And I am relaxed. So relaxed I feel like a cat basking in a patch of sunlight.

I stretch out on top of William and feel his hands move up my bare back.

"We should get up," I say, my voice hoarse from sleep.

"The hospital doesn't let visitors in until seven," he mutters drowsily. "It's still dark out."

I nuzzle into him further, inhaling his green apple scent.

"Still, we should be waiting outside to be the first ones in."

"This isn't Disneyland," William says, and I bite down on his neck. He's getting sassier by the second.

I love it. I want him to always talk back to me. It makes me horny.

I lean up on my elbows and stare down at him. He's deliciously rumpled, his sleepy blue eyes hooded and watching me.

"I want to be there when the doors open, William. Do not make me beg."

He rolls his lips between his teeth, making me wait. But finally, he utters, "Okay."

Well, that was too easy. I narrow my eyes at him. My entire life has been fighting with other people, even my ladies give me hell, but this man rarely pushes back.

I'm not sure I know what to do with that.

"You're not going to fight me on it?" I ask.

"No. I get it," he replies. "I know how much this means to you. Let's shower and grab some coffee and we can go."

"Is this a trick?" I ask, still baffled.

He lets out a small laugh. "No, come on, let's go break grandma out of jail."

I roll off the bed and tug him into the shower and then get on my knees and eat his ass for being so agreeable.

---

"Alright, Bren. Here is your walker. There is no need for you to go meandering about without it," I say, pulling the walker right up next to where she is perched on her sofa. The plants that were sitting on it have found a new home on the counter.

It took about an hour to discharge her from the hospital,

but we were able to get her home with no issues, and her doctor assured me multiple times she'd be alright.

Well, there are no take-backsies now, doc. I took a good long look at his name just in case I need to hunt this fucker down if something goes awry.

Brenda eyes the red walker, her neck still in that damn brace, and my heart constricts seeing her look so fragile. And tired. Like the fight has been sucked out of her.

Goddammit.

"You have everything you need right here. You don't even need to move. And Martha and Vikki are going to check up on you after we leave," I say and look over at my ladies who are scrolling through the TV and whispering to each other.

"Are you even listening to me?" I ask the two of them.

When they don't answer, I gently grab the remote from them and wield it in front of me in annoyance.

"Give that back, Lex," Vikki demands. But now it's my turn to ignore her.

"Will you check up on Bren?" I ask. "I need you to give me your word."

"We already said we would," Martha says with a roll of her eyes, like Bren didn't just break her fucking neck.

I mean, it is a small spinal fracture, but still, she broke something. And her wrist is sprained. And she looks fucking old as shit.

"And while I'm at it, you two need to be careful too. I couldn't stand one of you tumbling down. My heart can't handle it."

"No one is tumbling," Martha grumbles, holding out her hand for the remote. "I haven't tumbled in years."

I narrow my eyes at them and then slap the remote back into her palm.

"I want updates. Hourly."

"Yeah, yeah," Martha says, but I don't believe her because she can't find her cell phone and Vikki's has been dead for days. It's hopeless. They clearly aren't as worried about this as I am.

I am going to flirt with Ben at the front desk a little to get him to help me out. I am seriously reassessing my decision to not place cameras in their apartments. At the time I wanted to respect their privacy. I shouldn't have had such strict morals. I'll remember this for next time.

"Come here, Lex," Brenda says and I sink down next to her, grabbing onto her good hand and squeezing it gently.

"Don't worry so much. I'm fine."

"You are *not* fine."

She sighs and then rests her head against my shoulder.

"You need to stop worrying yourself so much. I've lived so very long, Lex. When I go, it will be okay. I've had such a good life, made only better by having you in it."

My eyes sting and I bite down so hard on my bottom lip that I draw blood. Because what the fuck is she talking about? This is not a eulogy, Brenda. Back away from the morbid talk.

"I am just so happy you have William now. You were so lonely before. Promise me you two will take care of each other."

I glance over at my man and see him watching us, his gaze a little watery.

Yes, so it's not just me. He's feeling something too.

"Yes, well I don't plan on ridding myself of him."

"He loves you," she says, her gaze meeting mine. "I can tell by how he looks at you. And you deserve it, Lex. You deserve him."

I glance away from her and sniffle, willing myself not to lose it right now. I need to be strong.

So I sit there, Brenda dozing on me, for what feels like hours until William approaches.

"We should go and let them rest," William says. "They're all napping."

I look over and see Vikki and Martha passed out, both of their mouths open slightly in sleep.

My eyes swivel to Brenda who has her eyes closed. I don't want to go. I want to hover all night long and keep watch. Like John Snow in the Night's Watch.

"Yeah, okay," I say and as I start to move away, Brenda startles.

"Are you leaving?" Brenda asks with a snort.

"Yes, but we'll be back tomorrow. Don't fall again in that time, Bren, okay?"

"I'll use my walker, I promise," she says with a smile. "Love you both."

I press into William, feeling his strength and just absorbing it.

"Love you too, grandma," William says.

"Love you, Bren," I manage to squeak out before William leads me out of the apartment. I lean my head against his shoulder and just breathe in his sweet scent. God, what the fuck would I do without him? What if he had never come home from Florida? What if he decided to live out there forever? I'm not sure I could manage the stress of this alone.

"I'm glad you're here," I tell him as we near the exit.

"Me too," he replies squeezing my hand gently.

As we near the check-in desk, I spot Ben. Swiping at my wet eyes, I quickly untangle my hand from William's and saunter over to the counter, placing my elbows on it and leaning forward.

"Hello, Ben-Ben," I say, smiling at him, forcing myself to flirt when really, all I want to do is be back in William's arms. But this is another means to an end.

"Hi, Lex," he says sweetly, his cheeks stained red. "What's up?"

"I was wondering if you could text me how Brenda is doing later today. It would be a favor I'd be happy to repay you for."

He looks away from me quickly and nods. "Yeah, um, sure I could do that."

I smile widely at him and reach over, tugging on his hair a little. His breath escapes him in a gasp, and I run a finger across his ear.

Need to make sure he feels motivated to follow through. I know how to hook them.

"Thanks, love," I say. "Look forward to hearing from you."

He flushes crimson and I turn around, looking for William, but he's not there.

I frown, feeling the absence of him acutely, and stride outside. The sky is turning grey and the air feels thick. It's fucking ominous, is what it is. Because this type of weather is unusual for summer in Southern California. Usually, it's sunny and hot. But the air feels wet, and I can smell the inevitable rain on the horizon. Must be a motherfucking monsoon.

In the distance I can see William leaning against his car, his arms folded across his chest, his eyes following me as I approach.

"Why the rush?" I ask, moving toward him, trying to wrap my arms around his waist, but he takes a step back.

"You were flirting. Right in front of me."

I roll my eyes and cup the back of his neck, pulling him toward me. I don't want him mad at me. I just want him to understand why I did it. I did it for *us*. And I can't take the distance between us right now. I *need* him.

"Don't be jealous, love," I say softly.

His eyes flash with irritation. "It's not that simple. How would you feel if I flirted with that guy or any guy?"

"But you don't flirt."

"Not the point, Lexington," he says sternly, and my dick jumps to attention. I love it when he gets all growly

I adjust my pants a little and shrug my shoulders. "It's not a big deal. I know who you want."

He narrows his eyes at me a little and then steps to the side, "Alright, then..."

But before he can move away, I pull him back into me, my hands digging into his arms.

"Don't you fucking dare. Not today. Not now. Please."

William's cheeks are flushed red, and I lean down pressing my lips to his. He groans against me, his mouth opening for me as he threads his hands through my hair.

God, I want him again. How is it possible that this desire for him has only grown stronger? I am desperate for him.

When our lips finally part, I cup his face in my hands. "I was wrong. I'm sorry, okay? I didn't mean it. I just wanted him to text me updates...I worry."

He presses his hands to my chest and pushes away from me gently. "Don't do that again, Lexington."

I rest my forehead on his and nod.

"Okay."

"I know you don't mean it, but it hurts me when you smile at someone else like you smile at me."

My eyes widen slightly and I cup the back of his neck.

"You're right. You're so fucking right. I'm sorry. It won't happen again."

He wets his lips and pulls me into him once more. "Come on. Let's go home."

I glance up at the sky and see a flash of light. A raindrop hits my cheeks and rolls down my neck.

"Yeah, let's get home. Traffic is a bitch when it rains."

———

"It never storms here in the summer," I say, pressing my chin to William's shoulder. We are standing in my apartment at the sliding door that leads to the balcony, watching the lightning split the sky. A low roll of thunder shakes the apartment complex and I press my lips to his neck, tasting him. Bubblegum. I want him in my mouth.

We're both dressed in athletic shorts and t-shirts, having changed into them after a frantic make-out session as soon as we got home. I went down on him as an apology for flirting with Ben.

I made him forgive me with my mouth.

"In Florida, it stormed a lot. It was so humid. I hated it," William says, arching into my touch. "I couldn't wait to come back home."

"Hmm, well, I'm glad you decided to. What would I do without you?"

"Same," he whispers.

A flash of lightning illuminates the sky once more and I bite down on his ear. He shivers a little in my arms and I slide my hands under his shirt, feeling how warm and alive he is.

"I could stand here watching this all night," he adds. "It's really beautiful."

"Me too," I say, not at all focused on the scene outside my window. No, I am completely focused on William who smells delicious and looks perfectly rumpled.

My phone buzzes against the counter and I pull away from William, letting my hand trail down his arm as I move toward the kitchen.

My eyes reluctantly leave his as I pull up my text messages.

**Diablo:** I would like to barter with you again.
**Diablo:** Let me know what I need to do.

Asshole wants me indebted to him again. He's always such a greedy fucker. He probably met someone at the game shop who had better miniatures than him and feels the urge to one-up them. I run a hand along my chin and glance over at William who is still watching the storm raging outside. I guess I could find something for Diablo to do.

Maybe hand him off some clients to work with.

A small chuckle escapes me.

That is a terrible idea.

Suddenly, my phone buzzes again and I glance down at it, expecting to see another text from Diablo.

But it's not. It's a call from Ben.

I fumble with the phone, pressing it to my ear, and I croak out a "hello?" The voice on the other end is soft and sorrowful. I know he's saying sentences but I can't understand.

"What?" is all I manage. "*What?*" I gasp.

And as my brain finally catches up and his words register, the phone suddenly slips from my hand and clatters onto the ground.

"Lexington?" William asks, moving toward me. But he

sounds worlds away. I'm underwater and I can't fucking breathe. My vision narrows and all I can do is feel William clutching onto my arms, trying to ground me, to hold me in place, but I am tumbling backward onto my ass on the kitchen floor.

No. *No, no, no, no.*

This is not happening. It can't be happening.

"We have to…" I gasp, feeling his hands on my shoulders. "We have to…"

I can't fucking breathe. My lungs no longer work.

"Shit," I hear him mutter, and then I'm swept into his arms and cradled against his chest. I tuck my face into his neck, breathing him in, trying to focus.

For a moment, I am pulled back to reality, but it's much too painful, so I allow myself to be swept away again. Because it's easier than dealing with the grief.

Dealing with the sorrow, with the regret.

I've lost so much in my life.

And now I've lost one more.

"It's okay. You're okay," William whispers, his lips on my temple. "Come back to me, Lexington."

I gasp, a wrecked breath entering my chest and I feel my cheeks damp with tears. I hear sobbing and realize it's coming from me.

It has to be a mistake. She was fine when we left. She was totally fucking fine. Maybe a little tired. A little resigned.

*Growing old is not for the faint of heart.*

My eyes snap open and I meet William's distraught expression. He must have picked up the phone and heard the news. He fucking knows. Tears stream down his cheeks and his breath comes out of his mouth in rasps and shakes. He squeezes me tighter to him, holding me, cradling me, as if he can make the pain go away using sheer willpower.

"We have to go. It—it's a mistake. It h—has to be a mistake," I stutter, my words broken and choppy.

"Yeah," he says, swiping his lips against my wet cheek. "Yeah. We can go. We can go anytime."

A loud rumble of thunder racks the apartment again and I cling to him, wanting to get up and move, but also not wanting to let go, to leave his embrace.

What if he leaves me too? What if I lose William?

I'd never recover.

Never.

I hold on to him a little longer, just feeling the way his chest rises and falls with heavy, broken breaths, just reveling in how alive he is in this very moment.

I finally take a deep breath and pull away and he takes that for what it is.

He moves out from beneath me and grabs my shoes, helping me toe them on, and then his arm is slung around me, half carrying me to the car because my legs don't fucking work. In the middle of the parking lot, they lock in place and refuse to move forward because I know what I'm walking toward, despite pretending like I don't.

William stumbles slightly, his body wrenched from mine. But we don't stay parted for long because I'm suddenly swept up in his arms and he's carrying me to his car.

I let him because I can't do this myself. I just can't face it.

Even though I know I have to.

As soon as we're on the road, I turn in on myself, pressing my forehead to the cold window and tucking my knees into my chest.

Without thought, I let it all tumble out. What are secrets

anymore anyways? Worthless pieces of information, really. William should know anyway. I should have told him ages ago.

"Leo, my brother, died when he was six," I say, staring blankly out at the rain. "I watched him go slowly. It was cancer. He was my best friend. He looked up to me, ya know? But I couldn't save him. He just got sicker and sicker, until he was too weak to fight anymore." I huff out a breath and close my eyes. "He was all I had and one day he was just gone. I feel like it's happening all over again."

William's foot lays off the gas a little and all I can hear are his steady breaths and the windshield wipers on the glass. Visions of my younger brother—his blond hair and his mischievous, crooked smile—invade my mind and I clench my eyes.

Fuck. I thought I was past it and had made peace with it. But I guess I haven't. It's why I fret so much over the ladies. Because I know what it's like to lose someone you love.

When my mom died, I gave zero fucks because she was an abusive piece of shit, but losing Leo tore something out of me.

I was never the same after that. There's been a lingering anxiety that has lived inside of me since he passed.

"Who's going to love me now that she's gone?" I whisper.

William reaches over and clasps my hand.

"Me, Lexington. *Me.* I will love you."

His silhouette swims before me and I hold onto him tighter. There have been so few people who have loved me as much as I loved them.

Brenda was one of them.

William will be another.

My William.

Brenda gave him to me. She knew she would have to leave

me someday, and so she chose to give me a piece of her to keep.

*Promise me you two will take care of each other.*

Fuck.

I let out a broken sob and stare at the swirling lights outside as we make our way through the storm.

This is so hard.

But I know I can get through it with him here with me.

I can do anything with William by my side.

# CHAPTER FIFTEEN

**WILLIAM**

Lex is not okay. The entire drive to the senior living facility he shrinks further and further inside of himself. The bright light inside of him is fading and I feel it acutely.

It's as if a bell jar has fallen upon us, sucking all the air out. He's stuck in his own head, his grief weighing him down. I know because I feel similarly. The only reason I'm still functional is because I have to be strong for Lex. We can't both fall apart. He needs me right now. He's counting on me, whether he realizes it or not, and I will be that pillar for him.

"Lexington," I whisper, putting the car in park, reaching over, and pulling him into my arms. I run a hand up his chest and feel his beating heart. It's erratic and my chest pinches.

I take a deep breath and steel myself.

"We're here," I say, and his red-rimmed eyes meet mine.

"I can't do it."

"Baby," I whisper. "We have to."

He swallows harshly, his throat clicking loudly. Outside, rain pelts the car, and we just stare at each other.

The utter wreckage of this moment completely envelops us.

"I forgot to ask, are you okay, love?" Lex asks, his voice hoarse.

My throat is sore and my eyes feel heavy but I smile sadly as I shake my head. "No, I'm not but I'm strong for you, Lex. I'll be strong for you."

He leans forward and pulls me into him, his lips seeking mine. When we pull away, he closes his eyes, steeling himself, and then quickly moves out of the car, stumbling slightly as he finds his footing. I jog up next to him, wrapping my arm around his waist, and he just leans into me.

"You don't have to be strong for me," he mutters, sniffling and swiping at his eyes.

"I want to," I tell him and press a kiss to his temple.

When we enter the lobby, I see Martha and Vikki waiting for us. Both look haggard and exhausted, eyes red-rimmed from crying.

"Lex," Martha says, sniffling loudly. "Come here, my boy."

Lex peels himself away from me and bends down to hug Martha to him. The embrace is long and drawn out and when she finally pats him on the back, he moves over to Vikki.

I just stand as an outsider, watching it all. And for a moment I feel lost. Because I was never a part of this found family. All I had was Grandma, and now that Grandma is gone, what does that make me?

I'm nothing to them.

Fuck.

I take a step back and Lex's head swivels toward me.

"Where are you going?" he asks.

I shake my head and wet my lips. "I want to give you privacy."

Lex frowns and then points to his side. "Come here, William. I need you."

I don't hesitate. I latch onto him, relieved.

When our hands are linked, Lex turns to both women and asks, "Where is she?"

"The funeral home is here...."

"Shit," he says and then swipes at his eyes. "We need to see her. One last time."

Martha and Vikki look at each other, silently communicating something, and then nod to the hallway leading down to the rooms.

Vikki holds onto Lex's arm as Martha marches ahead, and when we round the corner to her apartment, Lex sags into me.

Because there she is on a stretcher looking so fucking peaceful. Like she just closed her eyes and fell asleep. Her hand is on her chest and her lips are turned up slightly.

Like she's happy that it's over.

My god, my heart cracks a little and I blink furiously.

"William," Lex gasps, his grip on me bruising. "I can't. *I can't.*"

I pull him into me and once more, sweep him into my arms, cradling him to me as I walk to Martha's apartment.

I sink down on her couch as Lex sobs into my shirt, his tears soaking the fabric and wetting my skin.

Martha and Vikki sit down next to us, Martha's hand rubbing my back as Vikki holds on to Lex's hand as he shudders against me. I peek down at him and see his splotchy skin, red from crying. God, my heart. This is too fucking much.

I blink furiously, my chin trembling as I feel the comforting swirls Martha is drawing on my back.

"She was happy at the end and she went peacefully," Martha says after a moment of silence. "She went the way I want to go..."

Lex stiffens and lifts his head, his eyes a little duller than normal. "Don't do it, Martha. I can't bear it. I can't lose you too."

She pulls her bottom lip between her teeth and nods. "I have years left, asshole. I'll drink your fucking green tea. And I'll cut back on the sugar packets."

Lex lets out a wet laugh and then tucks himself back against me.

Vikki pats his hand and we just sit there in silence, our thoughts nearly as loud as the thunder rumbling outside.

"It is a bit ominous, the storm," Vikki says after some time and Martha scowls at her, swatting at her hand.

"Oh, for fuck's sake, Vikki, honestly. Now is not the time to joke about that."

"Well, she always said she would go out with a bang. I didn't think she meant it literally."

Lex turns his head and smiles softly.

"She did say that. She would always joke about it..." He inhales shakily. "Shit."

"Look, enough of this," Martha says, attempting to get off the couch but she gets stuck a little.

"Damn thing," she says. "I told my son that this couch was too low but he didn't listen. If you come to visit and can't find me, the couch probably ate me. Just check between the cushions with the loose change."

Lex helps her stand, and then she waddles out of sight, only to return a moment later with something in her hand.

"Are those my pajamas you've been working on?" Lex asks.

"You betcha."

He runs his hand over the fabric of the adult-sized footie pajamas and meets her gaze. "There are dicks on this. You used a dick pattern?"

"Yeah, so? You like cock."

He laughs and nods, and the sound is like a balm to my broken heart. "I do. Thank you, Martha."

"You're welcome," she says and then turns toward me. "Yours are coming, William. Don't be jealous. These things take time."

I squeeze Lex to my side and nod. "Thank you."

"So, what do we do now?" Lex asks with a sniffle.

"The funeral home will be in touch, and then we can plan for a memorial service...she told me what she wanted..." my voice cracks and Lex leans toward me, pressing his lips to my cheek.

"Don't cry, William. I mean, what the fuck am I saying? You can cry. Go ahead and cry, love."

And with those words, I just let myself crumble.

Lex's thumbs brush my tears away, and I just breathe him in, the essence of him permeating my soul.

"We have each other," he chants over and over and when I finally calm down, Lex is the only thing I can see.

"Don't leave me," I whisper.

"Never."

———

We make our way back to his apartment an hour later, and both of us are wrung out and exhausted. I have to almost carry Lex up the stairs and into bed.

Once we're inside, we strip down until we're both naked and we crawl into bed, our bodies sliding together, our hands on skin, just finding comfort in each other.

It doesn't feel sexual. No, this is desperation, pure and simple. A momentary escape from the pain. We wrap ourselves as tightly as we can around the other, our warm breath tickling our skin.

And that's how we fall asleep.

———

I spend the entire next day in bed with Lex. Neither of us bothers to dress and work is forgotten. Lex has rescheduled his clients and I let Jason know that I wouldn't be in the rest of the week.

He didn't even huff and puff like he usually does. He just muttered his condolences and hung up. It was all so eerily easy.

I run my hands through Lex's hair, feeling the puffs of breath against my shoulder as we hold each other. Neither of us is willing to be apart from the other for too long. At one point I got up to pee and Lex followed me into the bathroom, his eyes on me the entire time. And when he got up to grab a bottle of water an hour ago, I fidgeted nervously until he returned.

I can feel the absence of Brenda in my life acutely. It's as if a part of me has been carved out of me and I'm not quite sure what to do. How am I supposed to move on with life with her gone? I have no family now. I have no one but Lex. He seems to be the only solace from the pain in my chest. The only hope I'm clinging to.

I need him more than I've ever needed anyone.

It's not healthy, this codependence we have, or is it? Does it even matter? It's necessary. It's what we need. And whatever this is between Lex and me, it wasn't normal to begin with.

But normal is overrated in my opinion. And boring. And Lex is definitely not boring.

"Do you think she's happy now?" Lex asks, his hand sliding up my stomach. "Like in heaven or some shit?"

I inhale deeply. "Yeah. I do."

"Do you think she was happy here, with me? With us?"

I glance down at him and see his watery stare. "Of course she was."

"She looked so peaceful," he mutters and then shifts until he's completely on top of me, nuzzling his face into my neck, his hands sliding behind my back. "I think she knew it was coming soon. She hinted at it a lot. I shrugged it off and scolded her for it...but I think she was trying to prepare me. I just think there's no way to really prepare yourself for losing someone like that."

"Yeah, it's true," I say, running my hands up his sides and holding him against me.

We're silent a moment and he sighs. "I want to fuck you, William. Will you let me?"

He leans up and those sad eyes meet mine.

"Always."

"God, I love how you always say yes to me." He rests his forehead against mine. "I just want to feel something good, William. And you feel so fucking good."

I swallow roughly at the desperation in his voice and know that I need this just as much as he does. I pull him in for an intense and frenzied kiss, his fingers working me open, and then moments later he's sliding inside of me and fucking me deep and rough. We hold each other tightly, fingers clutching hard, digging in. I gasp as he runs his nails roughly down my chest and the physical pain mixed with acute pleasure feels so damn good. It drowns out the emotional pain and feels like a reprieve, like freedom.

I can feel him all the way to my soul.

There's something different about this time, something more needy, visceral, and powerful. Lex holds my gaze as he works me over the edge. I feel his cum unloading inside of me as I spasm around him, and then he collapses against my chest, panting wildly. I wrap my arms around him and kiss his forehead.

For a moment, I wonder if this is what making love feels like. We need to do that again when sorrow isn't hanging heavily over us.

"Fuck, I needed that."

"Me too," I say, kissing the top of his head. "Me too."

We lie like that for a while, his cock still buried inside of me, our sweaty bodies plastered against each other.

Finally, he sighs and pulls out of me. "We should go see Martha and Vikki. Maybe take them out for a healthy afternoon snack."

I groan, not wanting to move. I just want to fuck him again, to forget what happened last night. To pretend for a moment that my grandma is still alive.

But I know we can't do that. That's not how life works. And now Lex is looking at me with puppy dog eyes and I cave. He's right, I'll probably never say no to him.

"Let's shower and then we can go."

———

"I am showing restraint," Martha exclaims, only pouring three packets of sugar into her passion fruit iced tea. "Just for you."

Lex rolls his eyes and leans into me. He broke down once on the way over to pick them up but managed to dry his eyes as soon as we arrived. And now we are at a Starbucks a few blocks away, seated inside, just enjoying time with each other.

"I appreciate it, Martha, even though you ordered this extra sweet already."

"It tastes like linoleum without it, Lex. Don't harass me," she grumbles.

Lex sighs and glances over at Vikki who is looking guilty, her loaf of lemon bread mysteriously gone.

"Did you straight up eat that already? Seriously?" he asks, and I chuckle because I saw Vikki casually stick four cubes of butter on her frosted lemon bread and consume it like a Komodo dragon swallowing a goat when Lex wasn't looking.

She literally took two bites. For a moment, I was worried she'd choke but I guess the globs of butter helped it slide down.

"I love lemon bread and butter," she says, wiping at her mouth and taking a long sip of her iced coffee.

"Yes, well usually you spread the butter on thinly."

"Not me. I like it ice cold and in large chunks," Vikki says and then pats Lex's hand, and then she pulls an extra butter out of her purse and starts to unwrap it.

Lex slaps it out of her hand.

"Bad, Vikki," he says when she gasps at the butter now lying on the floor. "Four is good enough. And eating straight butter is disgusting."

She narrows her eyes at him and then lets out a laugh. "Fine. You're probably right. Five would be excessive."

"Honestly, you are going to give me grey hairs."

"Not like we could see them with your hair dyed like that," Martha chimes in, waving her hand toward Lex's silver-blond head.

"Yes, well they'll be there, even if you can't fucking see them."

"If you can't see them, they don't exist," Martha argues and Lex mutters something under his breath. I press a kiss to his cheek, hoping to calm him. He hasn't broken down since the car and I want to keep it that way. But grief is a funny thing. It hits you so unexpectedly, in the moments you least expect it.

"I miss her," Vikki says, her nose turning red, her eyes watering. "Fuck this getting old shit. It's depressing as hell."

"Well, we still have each other," Martha chimes in. "And I'm the youngest. I'll be the last to go."

Lex snorts at that and we all just sit there, eyes glassy with unshed tears, all trying like hell to not weep in the middle of Starbucks.

"And how are you doing William?" Martha asks. "How are you holding up?"

I roll my lips between my teeth and shrug, my eyes stinging. "It hurts. But having Lex..." my words trail off and I clear my throat.

Lex leans into me, his hand clasping mine. "Yes, we have each other now, love. You have me."

We finish our drinks and tote Vikki and Martha back to the facility before heading back to Lex's apartment.

At this point, I'm considering just asking him to let me move in. Most of my clothes are there anyway and I haven't been back to my apartment in days.

I know it's fast, but I want to do it. I've lived thirty years of my life without him. I don't want to spend another day away from him.

I'm about to bring this up, to just invite myself into his life when we step around the corner and I see Emery and August lingering outside of the front door.

Shit, I hadn't meant for them to come *today*. But then again, I'm not surprised. It seems as if Emery often gets mixed up. He must not have read my text message that carefully.

"Lexie," Emery says, pushing off the wall and pulling him into a smothering hug.

"Oh, fuck off, Eminem," Lex grumbles, but still wraps his arms around his best friend and buries his head in his neck.

For a moment, I bristle, but I let it go because he needs it, this friendship. I never had many friends, but the ones I've had meant a great deal to me.

I can only imagine what Emery is to Lex.

"Oh, do not take that tone with me. But I get why you're more rude than normal. I'm so sorry, Lex. William told us what happened."

Lex peeks over at me, his cheek resting on Emery's shoulder and his eyes soften. "Of course he did. He's a meddler. He learned that from..."

His voice cracks and he bites down on his bottom lip.

Fuck.

I can't stand seeing him cry again.

"Okay, now is the time to give him the food, August," Emery says. "Before he starts bawling. Because if he starts, I'll start. It will just turn into the great flood."

August holds out a dish covered in tin foil and we all eye it warily.

Lex pulls away from Emery and then raises an eyebrow at him.

"What did you do, Eminem?"

"I made you a casserole. I saw this in a movie. This is what people do, I think. I don't even know what the fuck a casserole is, so I improvised," Emery explains with a smile. "It tastes mostly okay, although it could be that August was lying to me to save my feelings. He does that a lot." He peers over at August and raises his eyebrows. "Were you lying to me?"

August stares at him, a small smirk on his handsome face. "I would never lie to you about something like this."

"Oh, I think you would," Emery mutters. "You never want to hurt me."

"Never," August replies.

"Well, whatever. Lies, truth, what does it matter? This casserole thingy is noodles and cheese and meat that is mixed together into something unidentifiable." He pauses and slaps a hand on his forehead. "Oh shit, you don't eat meat, do you, Lex? Fuck. Well, whatever. It's the thought that counts. Anyways, I think I may have forgotten an ingredient, but that's par for the course. Don't expect much from me, guys. I'm a mess. I did want to add Skittles to the mix because it really cannot get any worse and Skittles makes everything taste better, but August stopped me. He said, 'under no circumstances will you add that, Em' and it got me all hot and bothered. I love it when he uses his stern teacher voice on me. Makes me super horny."

My god, the rambling. I just stare at him, perplexed. And for a moment, I can feel the sadness recede because this is all so ridiculous.

Lex grabs onto the glass dish and stares at it, blinking rapidly.

I don't even know what to say. All I know is I don't want Lex to start crying again.

"Come in," I say loudly, wrapping an arm around him and unlocking the door. We step into the cool apartment and August and Emery follow right behind us.

As I put the casserole into the fridge, Lex sits down on the couch next to Emery, resting his head on his friend's shoulder. I suddenly decide that I need more caffeine. It's been a long ass day and even though my heart is already palpitating, my eyes feel heavy. I could lie down and sleep for the rest of the night.

Suddenly the thought to call my grandma pops into my head and I'm momentarily breathless. I realize I won't be able to call her ever again. The voice I'd come to love is gone forever. I'll never hear her say my name again, to tell me she loves me.

Fuck.

I lean against the counter and breathe deeply through my nose. My eyes sting as I watch the coffee spurt out of the machine and I will myself to keep it together.

I can let it all out tonight with Lex. When we're alone.

I glance over at him and see that he is listening intently to something Emery is saying and my heart stumbles.

Having him here with me makes it easier in so many ways. Neither of us is alone now.

"Let me help you," August says, moving in to grab two mugs from the counter.

His kind eyes meet mine and I blink up at him because Lex is right. August is disgustingly handsome. I can see why Lex felt so insecure about me potentially ogling him.

But he's not Lex.

Lex is in a league of his own.

I will never set my eyes on another.

I follow August back to the couch and sink down next to Lex who just crawls onto my lap and tucks himself against me, his mug cradled in his hand.

"So, tell me something disgusting about you two so I can take my mind off of all the bad shit going on," he says after a long silence.

Emery taps his lips before taking a noisy slurp of his coffee. Then he grimaces dramatically.

"There needs to be like ten more scoops of sugar in here. This tastes like soil and not the good kind."

"Is there a good kind of soil you eat?" Lex asks.

"There could be," Emery says while glancing back at August and holding out his mug. "Pretty please? Make it better. I cannot live like this. I feel like an earthworm drinking this."

August sighs and stands up, but before he moves into the kitchen he says, "Two scoops, Em. That's all I'm giving you."

"I mean, is this a negotiation? Because I feel like this is a hostage situation right now."

August chuckles lowly and moves into the kitchen, Emery's eyes on his boyfriend's ass as he goes.

Emery leans toward us. "Okay, so here is a little bit of gossip to hopefully take your mind off things."

Lex arches an eyebrow at his best friend. "Do tell. Don't skip any details."

"So, you know Diablo?"

Lex leans in closer and I find myself doing the same. Because I remember that little runt scurrying around Lex's apartment, stealing his food.

"So, get this, he called me today, and guess what?"

"What?"

"Apparently his dad is sending him away for safety reasons."

Lex leans back against me and sighs, "Damn, I was going to ask him to help me with my business..."

"Are you insane? That would be a huge mistake," Emery says. "He'd burn it to the ground. On purpose."

"True. I'm obviously not thinking clearly," Lex says and then asks, "What did that little shit do?"

Emery bobs his head and shifts in his seat a little. "Probably hacked the wrong person. He's always causing trouble. I tried to get the details, but he wouldn't fucking budge. Said it was a secret. I mean, can you believe him? Like I would ever say anything. I am a steel trap of secrets. Nothing gets out of me."

My eyebrows rise at that because that doesn't seem very accurate. He's more like a floodgate opened wide.

Lex sips at his coffee. "Is Skylar going with him?"

Emery bounces his leg and runs a hand through his hair. "Who the hell is Skylar?"

"Some super-muscular bodyguard that has been following him around for days now."

Emery stops wiggling for a moment and asks, "Is he hot?"

Lex shrugs. "If you're into titans."

I bite my lip to hold back a smile because I noticed Skylar too. How could you not? He's massive...and kinda scary, honestly.

Emery eyes August and sighs. "Nah, I like my man just as he is."

August looks over at that exact second and their eyes catch, a small smile lifting his lips before moving back toward the couch.

"Three scoops of sugar, just for you," he tells Emery.

Emery winces as he sips at it but still eyes us with a twinkle in his eyes.

"See? I got him to budge. He said only two scoops, but he gave me three."

August rolls his eyes but still pulls Emery back into his arms.

"So anyway, I got off track. And look, I know we just got here and you seem fucking tired, but I was thinking we could go out and do something. Take your mind off all this shit."

Lex sighs. "I'm not sure... I'm exhausted. It's been a long ass day."

"Oh yeah, totally, I get that. But I made you an appointment with my tattoo guy at seven. He can squeeze you in. I tried for your girl, but she's booked up. And I know you'd want to get something to remember Brenda. You texted me that font you like, remember? I think it would be perfect."

"Can I see?" I ask and Lex pulls out his phone, showing me a cursive font.

"This one. I want to get her name. I've been thinking about it all day."

I lean forward and press my lips to his temple. "That sounds amazing. If you're up for it, you should go."

Lex sniffles. "Yeah, it does. Okay, Eminem. Yeah. Let's do it."

When I meet Emery's gaze he smiles softly. "You could get one too," he tells me.

"I think I'm okay, thanks. As much as I love tattoos on Lex, they aren't really my thing."

"You're perfect without them," Lex says.

I press my lips to his, licking my way into his mouth, just enjoying the taste of him.

"Oh, for fuck's sake, this is making me anxious," Emery

mutters. "August, don't look. It's all very sexual. It's not for your innocent eyes. Although, it is giving me some ideas. I'm taking mental notes for later…"

We pull apart and Lex stares at his best friend. "I have literally seen you two fucking. There was nothing innocent about any of that."

Emery gasps. "You have not."

Lex arches an eyebrow and Emery waggles a finger at him.

"You better erase it. August is not for your consumption. He's mine. Do it now."

Lex lets out a soft chuckle and leans back against me, the sound resonating so sweetly in my ears.

"He's so fucking gullible."

"Asshole," Emery mutters, trying not to smile. "But I still love you. So, I'm not canceling this appointment with Hector. You're welcome. You can thank me with sugary lollipops."

# CHAPTER SIXTEEN

**LEX**

The tattoo gun whirls in the background as Hector bends over my wrist, inking Brenda's name into my skin.

William watches it all, his eyes wide, his fingers wrapped around my free hand.

I was fine driving over here, but now watching her name slowly appear on my skin is making my eyes sting. I worry if I start crying again, Hector will never let me live it down.

"Why you sniffling?" he asks, his eyes narrowed on me. "You sick? Because there is some bad shit going around and I'll be real mad if you infect me."

I roll my eyes and glower at him. It's better than sobbing.

"I'm emotional. It's a thing humans do."

Hector snorts. "You're just as sassy as Emery. That little shit."

"Yes, well we grew up together. We have similar tendencies."

Hector grunts and gets back to work. He wipes at the tattoo and I shift on the seat, the pain so familiar to me that it doesn't even bother me anymore. William leans toward me, whispering in my ear, "I love your tendencies."

And that L-word, it just pierces my heart and I suddenly remember him saying he'd love me now that Brenda is gone. I hadn't put much thought into it at the time. I was too lost in my grief. But now...

"Do you love me, William?" I blurt.

His forehead scrunches with confusion. "Have I not made that clear already?"

"Did you hear that, H? He can't even come out and say it," I say playfully.

"Yeah, that's a fucking red flag, my man," Hector says with a snort. "Where'd you find this one anyways?"

William rolls his eyes, muttering, "This isn't really the time or place."

"He's Brenda's grandson." I eye William and smile, feeling myself start to tear up again. "She gave him to me before she left so I wouldn't be alone. Told us to take care of each other."

Hector sighs uncomfortably and works a little faster because he's an emotionless asshole who doesn't want to hear my sob story.

A few minutes later, my new ink is done and William and I are walking outside. My chest feels uncomfortably tight and my eyes are on fire as I stare at my new tattoo, my forever reminder of Brenda.

Emery scampers over to us, his hair a little mussed, his cheeks flushed. Hmm, I have a feeling I know exactly what he was doing moments before. Actually, I know exactly what they were doing. I'm sure I'll hear all the details later. He can't help but brag about his sexy Mr. Rogers.

"Fuck, I almost missed you," Emery says, running a hand through his hair and then zipping up his fly. "Sorry. Got a little bored waiting around."

"Yes, well, I can tell," I say, eyeing him and Emery bounces from foot to foot. "Where is August?"

Emery waves his hand in front of his face. "He's getting situated. Enough about him. Let me see. I wanna see."

I bare my wrist to him and he bobs his head. "Looks super good. I mean, H is like the best at what he does. I keep trying to convert you..." His eyes meet mine and he nods. "Yeah, okay, I'm picking up on some cues here. I think you're telling me with your eyes that you want to go home."

"Finally learning how to read the room?"

"Yes, well, I never much liked reading, but I'm trying, okay," he says with a laugh. "August is teaching me things. And not just in the bedroom. He's very smart and emotionally intelligent."

"That he is," I say, and William tugs on my arm, trying to pull me away from this conversation. I'm glad because we're both exhausted and now that I don't have a distraction anymore, I'm feeling it.

The weight of our sadness.

I ache from it.

When we're back at the car, William stops and turns me to face him, looking into my eyes. He's silent for a minute and I raise an eyebrow, waiting for him to speak.

"I love you, Lexington. I know I don't say a lot, and voicing my feelings is not something I'm particularly used to. But I promise I'll work on saying it as often as you need. Just know that even when I don't say it, I feel it. All the time, every day."

Goddammit, this sweet man is going to be the end of me. I lean in, wrapping my arms around him, and hug him tightly, my stupid faucet eyes leaking again. Ugh, I can't cry anymore today. I refuse. Pulling back slightly, I meet his watery gaze and sniff. "Good, yes, well...now that that's cleared up, let's go home so I can bury myself inside you until we both pass out from exertion."

William chuckles and smacks me on the ass as I round the car, and in this moment, it feels just the tiniest bit easier to breathe.

———

## THREE DAYS LATER...

"Vikki, do not even with that. Fuck," I mutter, wrenching the large box from her arms. "I will be lifting the heavy shit. Or William, but not you. You are not a forklift, despite declaring that you are."

She rolls her eyes at me and I sigh. Because she is impossible. She's doing this just to mess with me, I know it.

Martha is sitting in a chair going through a Tupperware box of small souvenirs. She's being suspiciously quiet and amenable. She's plotting something, I'm sure. I need to check her pockets for items she may have stolen before she leaves.

We are packing up Brenda's things because someone else needs to move in at the end of the week. Just the thought of someone else inhabiting her space makes me want to break down and cry. I still can't believe she's gone, but with each passing day, it gets a little easier. It helps that William has let me be a part of the process, helping him plan a small memorial and going through her things.

I'm keeping some of this shit for me. William told me I could.

Her plants are already in my apartment and half dead from overwatering.

I need to give them a little space it seems. I'm smothering them with my love.

I glance over at William and my heart pounds erratically. It happens every damn time.

God, what would I have done if I hadn't had him with me through all of this?

Hell if I know. I wouldn't be doing nearly as well, that's for sure.

"If either of you falls and break something because you're being stubborn, William and I will be late to meet with the lawyer and I will be none too happy."

William smiles at me and I set the box down, moving toward him and pressing my lips to his. Because I just can't help myself.

"Are you sure you want me there?" I ask. The reading of the will is private and usually for family only. I really have no business attending, but when William insisted I was in fact family and needed to accompany him, I about melted right into the ground.

"I am one hundred percent sure," he says.

God, I love this man.

"I fucking love you," I blurt loudly, and William's eyebrows shoot up, obviously surprised at my brash and random declaration in the midst of half-packed boxes.

"Oh yeah?"

"Of course I do. I don't take this lightly. I've loved like a handful of people in my life, but I've never felt this way about another person."

His cheeks darken as he pulls me against him.

"Well good, and I love you too."

"Yes, I know that already because you've told me a thousand times already." He blushes even deeper, and I lean into him to whisper, "I especially like it when you scream it while I'm fucking you."

"I don't scream," he hisses, and I push away from him with a laugh.

"Yes, you do. You just do it very quietly. I fucking like it, but enough about that. Chop, chop. We have to get this shit done before we leave." My eyes fall on Martha who is pilfering some fabric and knitting needles that Brenda had stored away in one of her bins. She's stuffing it all under her shirt.

I just turn a blind eye. As long as she keeps making me pajamas I'll pretend like I don't see. Brenda would have wanted her to have it anyways.

———

The old lawyer that Brenda entrusted with her estate looks to be about three thousand years old. His skin has the constitution of wax paper, and he has an old friar haircut. He's straight out of a twelfth-century Parisian town and looks like he should be carrying a scroll and shouting about the monarchy.

"This whole place is spooky. I cannot believe Brenda trusted this man. She was obviously delusional toward the end. He looks like he took part in the Inquisition."

William looks around the dark space. "Yes, it's a bit vampiric, isn't it."

"More like a creepy necromancer. I guarantee you that

man is older than he looks. He probably brought himself back from the dead," I utter as we approach the lawyer's desk.

I shudder as I take in his plain suit and then move my eyes to the decorations: dark wallpaper, sagging bookshelves, and to my horror, a tiger rug that spans half of the floor.

"I don't think that rug is fake," I whisper to William. "He probably skinned it alive back when he was a caveman."

William huffs a laugh as he sinks down into an antique leather chair. The entire thing squeaks loudly.

"Keep it together, Lexington," he tells me with a chuckle, and I don't even bother sitting in my own chair. I just plop right down on his lap. It's safer this way. Two against one. I am pretty sure I could take this creep.

The lawyer startles slightly at how we chose to sit, but I ignore him. Back when he was born, in medieval times, men had to do this in hiding. It's the twenty-first century, asshole. If you don't like it, go back to the Renaissance.

The lawyer starts to prattle on and on, regurgitating some legal jargon that bores me to tears. I'm only half listening, just fiddling with William's hands and smelling him. He's delicious. He smells like peach cobbler today. I don't know how he manages it. It's fucking ridiculous. The day he stops smelling like dessert is the day I die.

"Half will go to Lexington Cavanaugh and the other half to William Walker," the lawyer says.

My entire body freezes because my brain just caught up to what was said. "Excuse me?" I ask, confused. Because what the fuck is he talking about?

"Half to Lexington and half to William," the zombified man repeats.

I shake my head. "Half of what?"

"The inheritance. The estate."

"Well, I don't fucking want it," I say, feeling my eye start to twitch. Because there is no way William is going to be happy about this. That's the whole reason he didn't trust me in the first place. He thought I was after Brenda's money.

"*I don't fucking want it*," I hiss, trying to stand up, but William's arms wrap around me, tugging me back against him.

"Lexington," he says softly, but I'm getting so worked up over this that I stop thinking clearly. My ass swivels in his lap and I turn and face him. He needs to see my fucking eyes when I say this. To understand how sincere I am about this.

"Listen to me, William. I don't want it. I'd rather keep you instead. I was never here for the money. You have to believe me."

"I know. I *know* that. But you can have both. She wanted you to have half. She loved you. So you should take it. And you'll always have me. Always. This doesn't change anything."

I slide my lip ring into my mouth and shake my head. I want to convince him otherwise, but he's just as stubborn as Brenda was.

"Fine. Fine. I'll take the fucking money. Just know that I have my ways of giving it all back without you knowing."

William rolls his eyes and squeezes me against him.

"And," I add, "I want you to continue to love me. Money has a way of getting between people. You have to promise me that."

"Yes. I promise. I'll love you no matter what," he says and my heart skips a beat.

"We'll see."

William presses his face into my neck and sighs against me.

"There's nothing to see. We can discuss the money later."

He lowers his voice so only I can hear. "Let's just agree so we can leave. This guy is creeping me out."

I eye the lawyer who hasn't blinked once since we entered his office thirty minutes ago and agree.

Yes, William, good point.

It's best to leave the vampire lair before he sucks our blood.

"Fine, what do we have to do?"

The lawyer drones on and on, unable to do anything with precision before he leans forward and I swear I see his skin slip down his face.

He must be wearing a skin mask over that skeleton of his.

"She left you both letters," the undead man says.

And time stops. Utterly stands still. My breath comes out in a whoosh and I begin to tremble because I wasn't expecting this.

"Can we have them?" William asks, reaching past me, his hand shaking slightly.

The man holds them out to us and I grab mine, clutching it to my chest, my eyes wet and my throat sore.

"I'll read it when we get home," I tell William, who has already opened his letter and has consumed it.

I won't be doing that. I am going to read it slowly and savor every word.

That night, when William is sound asleep, I steal out into the living room, curl up on my sofa and open the letter.


*Dear Lex,*

*My sweet boy. The moment you walked into my life you were mine. I want you to know that I see you as my son, my grandson, a part of my heart. I love you dearly and have so enjoyed getting to know what a wonderful, bright, and caring man you are. So, take heart, be brave,*

*and hold onto hope. You will find love again once I'm gone. You have*
*been loved by me and you will be loved again by another.*
*You deserve the world, Lex.*
*Thank you for letting me be a part of yours.*
*Love always,*
*Brenda.*

# EPILOGUE

*SIX MONTHS LATER*

**LEX**

"That looks fucking ridiculous on you," I tell William who shifts on his feet in the middle of our living room wearing a shirt that Martha made him.

"I *have* to wear it. She made it."

I raise an eyebrow at him and then try to smother a laugh but fail. Because Martha would, the saucy minx.

"It has my face all over it. You're wearing a Lex shirt."

William runs a hand down his chest and his cheeks turn strawberry pink. "Yes, she's very inventive."

"I think she special ordered the fabric and then made this to see if you'd actually wear it. It's a test, William."

"Yes, well, I am. I can't not wear it."

"Very true," I say, sliding a finger down his arm and

watching as goosebumps prickle his skin. He's still not tired of me, still as insatiable as ever, and he tells me he loves me every day. He gave up his apartment and moved in with me shortly after the funeral, and honestly, I've never been happier. I've finally found my person, my home, and I'm never letting go. He's stuck with me now.

"Well, I love it. I like that people can see who you belong to."

He huffs and I pull him in for a filthy kiss.

"Now, as sad as this makes me, we have to go. We have to get Vikki and Martha and take them to get their pedicures. The place does not tolerate tardiness."

And let me tell you, I researched the fuck out of nail salons that were actually sanitary. This place costs an arm and a dick, but I'll pay it because they sanitize their tools properly.

I also convinced William to get his nails done and I, of course, will be getting the full treatment.

"I don't know why you even bothered. Vikki is just going to grumble the whole time and Martha is going to try to make away with the nail polish."

"Yes, well, we have to be very vigilant, love."

William leans into me and wraps his arms around my waist.

"Fine, but I'm only doing this for you."

"Oh, I know it, William. You never say no to me."

I am so sorry I killed Brenda, but she had to go. Maybe that's why I had such a hard time writing this. I didn't want to do it.

Anyways, who should come next? Colin or Diablo?

Choices, choices.....

# ACKNOWLEDGMENTS

First, I would like to thank my editor, Angela O'Connell, for all of your hard work on this book. I always love your suggestions. They only make the book better. Thank you for putting up with me.

Thank you to my alpha reader Lark Taylor for taking time out of your busy schedule to read this. And reassuring me that it is, in fact, not garbage.

Margaret Neal thank you for beta reading this while on vacation and picking out the lingering mistakes we all missed. You are amazing.

And last, but not least, thank you to all the readers who continue to read my books and reach out with encouraging words. It keeps me writing.

# ABOUT THE AUTHOR


Cora Rose loves any kind of romance and consumes way too many books each year. She currently lives in the U.S. and spends her days daydreaming about the characters inside her head.

You can reach her on her website or email her at Cora-RoseRomance@gmail.com

# ALSO BY CORA ROSE

The Unexpected Series

Whit

Sem

Emery

Luke

Lex

Colin

Diablo

The Inevitable Series

Until Him

Always Him

Standalone

Waiting for You

Unlucky 13

Exception